# *Tryout Day*

"Patti? Are you awake? It's tryout day."

My eyes popped open. My little sister, Missy, stood over my bed.

Tryout day—the day I'd been thinking of ever since last July in Texas when Mom first showed me the flyer about the clinic, ever since I heard those words *the Paxton cheerleaders*.

I headed for the bathroom, wondering: If I'd known everything that was going to happen— all the ups and downs and tears and making up—would I still have wanted to try out?

Like we used to say back home—you bet!

# THE PAXTON CHEERLEADERS™

# Go For It, Patti!

## Katy Hall

A Parachute Press Book

A MINSTREL® BOOK

PUBLISHED BY POCKET BOOKS

New York   London   Toronto   Sydney   Tokyo   Singapore

A MINSTREL PAPERBACK *Original*

A Minstrel Book published by
POCKET BOOKS, a division of Simon & Schuster Inc.
1230 Avenue of the Americas, New York, NY 10020

Copyright © 1994 by Parachute Press, Inc.

ISBN: 0-671-89790-X

First Minstrel Books printing August 1994

10  9  8  7  6  5  4  3  2  1

PAXTON CHEERLEADERS is a trademark of Parachute Press, Inc.

A MINSTREL BOOK and colophon are registered trademarks of Simon & Schuster Inc.

Cover art by Cliff Miller

Printed in the U.S.A.

*for Tara Torpey*

# CHAPTER 1

*The Paxton cheerleaders.*

I'll never forget the first time I heard those words. It was on a Saturday morning in July. I had on my Dallas Cowboys T-shirt and a pair of white shorts, and I was sitting at our kitchen table spreading strawberry jam on a slice of toast.

That's when my mom broke the news.

"Moving?" I said. "Us? Out of *Texas?* No way!"

Mom sat across from me at the round oak table and nodded. "This promotion is a big chance for your father, honey," she explained. "He'll be head of copy machine sales all over the Midwest. It's a once-in-a-lifetime opportunity."

"But what about *my* life?" I wailed, folding my arms on the table and dropping my head onto them.

"Patti! Where's your spunk?" Mom reached over and gave my braid a little tug. "You and Missy and Daddy and I are going to *love* living in Paxton. You'll see. It's such a sweet little town, right on a

1

lake, and it's close enough to Chicago so we can zip in for day trips. And just think, Patti—this winter you and Missy will get to experience *real* snow!"

They don't call my mom Sunny for nothing.

They call me Patti, but my real name's Patrice. (It is *not* Patricia.) I'm almost thirteen, going into seventh grade. I'm five feet tall, and I almost always wear my hair in a braid. I've got my mom's coloring—my hair's blond and my eyes are blue—but on the morning Mom told me the news about moving, they were also *red* from crying.

After a while I lifted my head from the table. "Is this job why you and Daddy went up to Chicago last month?" I asked.

Mom nodded again. "I didn't want to tell you and Missy about it until it was a sure thing. And now it is."

"But I'll have to start a new school!" I wailed.

"Paxton Junior High," Mom said happily. "It's a *wonderful* school, honey, and *all* the seventh graders will be new."

"But what about cheerleading? What about tryouts for the Belton Middle School squad? I'm supposed to be Melody's partner!"

"Maybe this will cheer you up," Mom said, handing me a bright yellow flyer. "I phoned the cheerleading sponsor at Paxton Junior High, Mrs. Holland, and she sent me all the information."

The flyer said:

2

## PAXTON JUNIOR HIGH SCHOOL
## CHEERLEADING CLINIC!
A free clinic for seventh-grade cheerleading hopefuls
will be held in the PJHS gym
from 9:00–3:00 on August 12–14
***Bring a lunch!***
The junior high and high school cheering squads
will teach routines and provide individual help!
Cheerleading tryouts will be held on Saturday,
August 29.

"Doesn't that sound like *fun?*" Mom squeezed my hand.

"But Mom!" I cried. "The kids in Paxton aren't going to vote for me in their cheerleading elections! I'll just be some . . . some girl from Texas that nobody knows!" I started biting my left thumbnail.

"Now, Patti, honey," Mom began, "the Paxton students want the best cheerleaders to represent their school, and I just know that you'll be one of the best! Of course they'll vote for you!"

I groaned and switched to biting my right thumbnail. How could Mom even *think* kids would vote for me?

"Mrs. Holland told me that the eighth- and ninth-grade cheerleaders are chosen in the spring," she was saying, "but they save six spots for incoming seventh graders. Oh, honey, I know you're going to miss trying out for the Belton squad, but who knows? Maybe this fall you'll be one of the Paxton cheerleaders!"

*The Paxton cheerleaders.* When I heard those words, something inside me clicked. Of course I hated the

3

thought of moving. Hated it! But, I thought, if I could become a Paxton cheerleader, then maybe—just maybe—I'd survive the move.

My mom *would* check out the cheering situation. She had been a big cheerleading star at the University of Texas—she was co-captain of the squad. The other co-captain was her identical twin sister, Peggy. The University of Texas is where my mom met my dad, too—Bill Richardson, the team's star quarterback.

We've got a photo album labeled *Wild Bill* with a big 23 on the cover, which was the number on my dad's football jersey when he played for U.T. and for the five years he played for the Dallas Cowboys. It's full of pictures of what my dad jokingly calls his "glory days."

We've got another album labeled *Sunny & Peggy*. It has zillions of photos of the blond, ponytailed twins doing double-hook jumps and cartwheels at the games. Back then, Mom and Aunt Peggy were the best. But of course cheering has really changed. It used to be girls rooting for guys on a team. But not anymore. Now, with cheering competitions getting so popular, it's more like a team sport. We do flips and walkovers and handsprings—really hard stunts—just like gymnasts. And it takes teamwork. Not to mention trust. Plus we do these great dance numbers. Boy, wind me up and I could talk about cheerleading forever!

But what I couldn't do right after I heard we were moving was eat. To Mom, skipping breakfast is worse than not having any school spirit, but on that morning she didn't say a word when I got up from the table and headed for my room.

4

Walking through the door, I realized that what I'd called *my room* for twelve years wouldn't be my room much longer. I sat down at my desk, staring up at the big bulletin board above it. On that bulletin board was the history of my life so far.

In one corner was a bumper sticker that said BORN TO CHEER. Sometimes I think I was. I was in *diapers* when Mom took me to *Three Cheers for Baby!* Mrs. Estrada took Melody, too. Melody's my best friend. It was pretty much like a toddler tumbling class, I guess, except that we Cheer Babies got to run around waving little pompons. And instead of learning nursery rhymes, we learned yells.

Beside the bumper sticker was a picture of me, four years old, in the miniature red-and-white cheerleading outfit that I wore when I was the mascot for the Belton High cheering squad. Next to that—me again, this time in a blue-and-white skirt and sweater, doing a cheer for the Little League Dolphins. And here I was in my Dolphins baseball uniform, when, for a couple of years, I decided I'd rather play second base than cheer. In one game I hit a grand-slam home run, and I still kept that old home run softball on my desk.

The next picture showed Melody and me doing toe-touch jumps at a sixth-grade basketball game. In fourth, fifth, and sixth grades she and I were on our grade school cheering squad. Then we were too young to do pyramids and other really cool partner stunts, and we all looked forward to the day when we'd be old enough to try out for the big time—the Belton Middle School squad. And now I was old enough. And now I was moving!

I flopped down on my bed. If I could make cheer-leader, I thought, at least I'd know the other girls on the squad when school opened. But what if they did jumps I'd never even heard of? What if I couldn't do them? And even if I could, so what? There was no way kids in Paxton would vote for me! It wouldn't be like Dallas, where I had plenty of friends, and where being the daughter of a Texas cheerleading legend meant some-thing.

When I saw tears falling on my pillow, I realized I was crying. I put my head down then and just let myself cry.

# CHAPTER
## 2

**G**o for it!" squawked Petey, our little green parakeet. His cage hung just inside the family room door. We always practiced cheers in the family room, and Petey had picked up the basics.

"Hi, Petey," I said as I trudged glumly into the family room later that afternoon, still feeling teary. I plopped down on the couch and started biting my pinky nail.

"Hi, honey," Mom said softly. She was sitting at the table, doing some paperwork. "Feel better?"

"No."

"Well, you will." Mom smiled. I could tell she planned to act supercheerful until she had me smiling again. "Did I tell you that the Paxton Lions' colors are blue and yellow?"

"Ewwww," I said. I preferred being true to Belton's red and white.

"Patti!" exclaimed Mom. "Blue and yellow are *fantastic* together!" She looked thoughtful for a moment, then she popped up from the couch. "I was saving this as a surprise, but maybe now is the perfect time for it. I'll be right back."

A minute later she reappeared in the doorway. "Ta-da! How's this for making a good impression at the cheering clinic?"

In one hand she held the cutest little royal blue short skirt I ever saw. It had about a thousand pleats, and somehow it just looked peppy, even on a hanger. In her other hand was a bright yellow T-shirt. I had to admit it—side by side, blue and yellow did look great.

"Now check these out," Mom said, tossing me a bright blue baseball cap with a yellow *P* on the front and pair of white socks with a tiny blue paw print on each ankle. "They're lion prints."

"They're great," I said. Her plan was working. I was cheering up. I ran over and gave her a big hug. "Where'd you get all this stuff?"

"From my cheerleading catalogs." She beamed me a big Sunny smile. "I'm so glad you like the outfit, honey!"

An hour ago I'd been sobbing my heart out because my life was ruined. But now, seeing this cheery blue-and-yellow outfit, I could halfway imagine putting it on and doing a few handsprings for the Paxton Lions.

If I was good enough to make the squad. If they didn't cheer too differently up in Indiana. If kids at Paxton Junior High were willing to vote for someone they didn't know. If, if, if . . .

"We're home!" boomed my dad's voice.

"Back here!" Mom shouted in the direction of the front door. "Come see what we're doing!"

8

On thing about us Richardsons—we all have superloud voices.

"Mommy!" cried Missy as she zoomed through the family room door and took a flying leap into Mom's arms.

"Ooof!" puffed Mom as she made the catch.

Missy's real name is Melissa, but no one ever calls her that. She's tiny for her age, which is seven, and she has white-blond curly hair. She cannot hold still for more than two seconds and she's a major motormouth, always asking questions, which can drive me *crazy*. But once when Aunt Peggy asked Missy what she wanted to be when she grew up, she said, "Patti." I try to remember that when she starts in with her questions.

Missy and my dad had spent the morning at a Little League softball game where Missy was cheering for the Jackrabbits. She was still dressed in her little blue-and-white skirt and top.

"Hey, Patti-cakes!" Dad said, using his nickname for me.

My dad's got brown hair, cut short. He seems big to me, but for a football player, he isn't. Quarterbacks, he's explained, don't have to be huge. Just speedy. But even though he was fast, he did get tackled. That's how he got his nose broken—five times. His face is still a little lopsided, in a handsome way.

"Hi, Daddy," I said. "How was the game?"

"Good," he answered, before he kissed Mom hello. "But not this good." He wrapped both arms around Mom and kissed her again.

"Who won?" I asked, hoping that my parents weren't

going to get too mushy right in the middle of the day. When they start kissing, they're so embarrassing!

"The Jackrabbits," Missy said. "Six to two."

"Did you try the new jump I showed you?"

"Sort of," said Missy. "But guess what, Patti—Daddy told me we're moving to Paxton next week!"

"Not quite next week, Missy," said Dad.

"In about four weeks, honey," said Mom. "Now Bill, you and Missy come and look at Patti's new outfit."

As they admired my clothes, I thought: *Four weeks.* Sunlight streamed into the family room right then, and as I looked around I had a feeling just how fast those weeks would fly. I wanted to memorize this room, this moment, this feeling of happiness so that I could bring it back some snowy day in Paxton, Indiana.

*"Go!"* Petey cried from his corner. *"Go! Go!"*

"We're going, old bird," I told him. "Don't rush us!"

"I can't wait till you girls see our new house!" Mom said as Dad pulled our white van out of our driveway at dawn on moving day morning. "It sits way up on a hill in Berkshire," she went on, "which is the prettiest subdivision you ever saw. You'll each have your *own* bedroom, and," she added, "there's an extra room—a mystery room!"

From that moment on, while I tried to tune in to decent stations on my portable radio, Missy bounced around in her seat, asking about that room. "What's *in* the mystery room?" she wanted to know. "Can't you just give us a clue? Is it big? Is in down in the basement? Is it scary? Is it funny? Will I like it? Will Patti like it more than me? Can we all fit in it at once?"

The drive from Texas to Indiana took three days, and on the evening of the third day, by the time we reached the sign saying

WELCOME TO PAXTON
## Pop. 21,605

Mom didn't look so sunny anymore.

"They'll have to change that sign," Dad remarked as we passed by. "Make it say twenty-one-thousand, six-hundred nine."

"Our electricity won't be on until tomorrow," said Mom, who was driving, "but I think there's enough daylight left for you girls to see the house."

"Yay!" shouted Missy. "We're going to see the mystery room!"

And so, instead of heading straight for the motel, at the next intersection Mom turned between a pair of iron gates with iron letters spelling BERKSHIRE. We drove up a hill—past dozens of houses. Finally Mom stopped in front of a mailbox with 23 painted on it and said, "We're home!"

"Look, it's my old football number," joked Dad. "Now you know why we *really* bought this house."

Mom turned off the car, leaned over, and kissed my dad.

"Oh, brother," I said as the kissing continued. "Come on, Missy, let's go check it out."

We hopped out of the car and ran up the front walk. The house looked like one a kid in kindergarten might draw: a two-story red brick with dark green shutters and

11

a chimney. It had a nice yard around it, too, with big trees.

"Hurry up!" Missy called back to Mom and Dad.

Finally Mr. and Mrs. Kissy-face got out of the car and raced up the walk. When they reached the front door, Missy pressed the doorbell about twenty times while Dad unlocked the door.

"Follow me," said Mom as we walked inside.

Our footsteps echoed through the empty rooms. At the far end of the dining room Mom opened a glass-paneled door.

"Here's the mystery room!" she announced, and stepped aside.

Missy and I ran in and gasped. The room was huge! It had polished wooden floors, like a gymnasium, and mirrors covered two whole walls. Above the mirrors narrow windows went right up to the ceiling, and a row of skylights showed the sunset sky.

"Wow! Wow! Wow!" cried Missy, sounding like an excited puppy. She began turning cartwheels, and I followed right behind. In that room it seemed impossible *not* to turn cartwheels. What a perfect place to practice cheering, I thought.

"Isn't it great!" Mom turned a cartwheel herself.

"Show-off!" I teased her. "What's this room for, anyway?"

"The couple we bought the house from added this studio onto the house so their daughters could have private ballet lessons," explained Mom. "That was their practice barre." She pointed to the waist-high wooden railing along one wall. "It'll be perfect if I decide to give aerobics classes."

"What do you call this room?" asked Missy.

"The gym," said Dad.

"But it's prettier than an old gym," I said.

"The fitness center?" suggested Mom.

"Yuck." Missy wrinkled her nose.

"Well, what do *you* call it, Miss?" Mom asked.

"I," said Missy, "call it the cartwheel room."

And even though we tried for a while, we never could seem to call it anything but that.

# CHAPTER 3

*H*i, Petey!" Missy squealed the next morning as she danced in circles around the mover who held the birdcage, nearly tripping him. "I missed you, little birdie!"

As more and more movers began carrying things into our new house and as Missy kept jumping up and down, trying to see everything, Mom took me aside.

"How would you like to earn ten dollars by keeping Missy out of the way?" she whispered.

"Deal," I said. "Hey, Missy!" I called, grabbing my radio. "Let's go hang out in the cartwheel room."

"Cool!" said Missy, and off we went.

The mirrors in the room now reflected our plants, making it look as if we had twice as many. Petey's cage hung in the corner where the mirrors met. When I brought him some fresh water and filled his seed cup, Petey was already bobbing his head to the pair of mirror birds, saying, *"Go, Bulls!"*

"What do you want to play?" Missy asked me. "Cheerleading Camp? Or Coach and Cheerleader?"

There wasn't much difference between these two games that Missy had cooked up. Either one would give me a chance to practice cheering, which was what I wanted to do anyway.

"Camp," I answered.

"Okay," said Missy. "I'm the camper and you're the very strict counselor."

"Right." I twisted the radio dial to find something with a good beat. "Stretch out, camper," I said. "And no bouncing!"

Missy and I sat down on the floor, facing each other, and stretched our legs out to the sides as far as we could. After that we did shoulder rolls, head rolls, and arm circles.

"Okay, camper," I said, "let's raise some spirit!"

Missy and I faced the long mirror, our hands on our hips. "Let's do 'Hey, you!' " I said. "Ready? *And!*"

> *Hey . . . you! Out in the crowd!*
> *If you've got spirit, clap out loud!*

We clapped ten times, then yelled, "Hey!"

"Not bad, camper," I told Missy.

"Thanks!" said Missy. "Now let's play Coach and Cheerleader. I'm the cheerleader and you're the very strict coach."

And so the morning passed in the cartwheel room.

Around noon Dad came in with some sandwiches. "How's the practice going?" he asked.

"Great," Missy told him.

"Speaking of practice," he said, throwing in some big pillows for us to sit on, "you girls know the joke about the man who got lost in New York City?"

"Yes!" Missy and I cried together.

"Well," Dad continued, ignoring us, "the lost man goes up to this other man on the street and says, 'Excuse me, how do you get to Carnegie Hall?' And the other man says ...'"

" 'Practice, practice, practice!' " We all recited the punch line together.

Missy and I booed the joke loudly, and I heaved one of the pillows at Dad's head. He ducked out of the room, laughing. When it came to awful old jokes, Dad was the all-time champ.

I'd heard that joke for years before I found out that Carnegie Hall really *is* this big-deal concert hall in New York City. Some musicians and singers really do spend their lives practicing so they'll be good enough to "get to Carnegie Hall."

After we ate, Missy and I lay around on the pillows, listening to the radio and giving our lunch time to settle. I checked out my nails. Nine looked okay. The whole trip north I'd tried not to bite them, but I kept catching myself doing it. So I'd decided to compromise by chewing only on my thumbnail.

"Patti?" said Missy. "You think you'll make cheerleader?"

"I hope so, Missy." Suddenly my lunch started feeling sort of bubbly in my stomach. "I don't want to talk about it, all right?"

"But what if they don't cheer the way you do?" she asked.

"Are you a mind reader?" I cried. "That's *just* what I'm worried about! I have no idea how they cheer in Paxton!"

"But what if you *don't* make it, Patti?" Missy insisted.

Groaning, I fell back on my pillow. "If I don't make it, Missy, I will take a vow of silence. Not one word will pass my lips, ever again. All the kids at Paxton Junior High will ask me my name, but I won't be able to tell them."

"Because of the vow of silence," said Missy.

"Right," I said, scooting closer to my sister. "And I will become thin and pale and . . . very ghostly."

Missy's eyes were wide.

"Like a ghost, I will wander the hallways, silent and alone, and become known as the . . . SCHOOL SPIRIT!"

With that I jumped on Missy and tickled her like crazy.

"Now *you* take a vow of silence!" I said.

"Okay," said Missy. "But Patti?"

"Now what?"

"I hope you make it."

For the next few days all we did was unpack. I loved my new room. It had blue-and-white-striped wallpaper and was so big! The bathroom that Missy and I shared was big too, with an old-fashioned tub that stood up on little clawed feet.

Dad helped me shove my white wicker furniture around until we found just the right arrangement. Then I unpacked my clothes and books and put all my pictures up on my bulletin board. When I set my old home run softball on my desk, my new room started to feel like my old room.

One afternoon Mom drove us to the Paxton Mall. She said we could pick out whatever we wanted for our bedspreads and curtains. Everything I picked out was white—even a little white rug. I could tell Mom was dying to tell me how impractical and dirt-gathering white was, but she managed to keep her promise and let me choose. She didn't even say a word when Missy picked out a bedspread with a fat pink pig on it!

"I love piggies," Missy announced as we left the linen store. "Don't you, Patti? Don't you love piggies?"

"With all my heart," I told her.

Driving back home, Mom said, "Oh, look, Patti, over to your right. That's Paxton Junior High, where you'll be for the clinic tomorrow."

Tomorrow! After just one look at the big brick building with a long gym attached, I bit off two fingernails in record time.

"Do I look okay?" I asked as I came down the stairs the next morning a little after eight, wearing my yellow T-shirt, little blue skirt, and blue baseball cap.

"Whooo-eeee!" whooped Mom. She stood at the bottom of the stairs, holding a cup of coffee. "You look fantastic!"

18

"I'm so nervous, Mom!"

"Nervous? It's those *other* girls who should be nervous. Wait till they see that toe-touch jump of yours. Now come have a good breakfast, and then I'll drive you over to the clinic."

"Can't I go, too?" Missy begged in the van. "Please!"

"We'll find you a place to cheer in Paxton, Missy," Mom promised. "But today's Patti's day." She smiled over at me.

We made a quick stop at a deli, and I picked up a turkey sandwich and a lemonade for my lunch. I wrote my name on the bag the best I could as the car lurched along.

My family has a superstition about last-minute good luck wishes, sort of like theater people who wish each other the worst by saying "Break a leg." Mom pulled up outside the junior high, and her advice to me as I got out of the van was the very *last* thing you'd ever tell a cheerleader.

"Don't smile," she said.

I walked swiftly toward the entrance of the gym, opened the door, and walked in. I stopped. There's been a mix-up, I thought. This can't be a cheerleading clinic. For everywhere I looked, I saw girls in cutoff jeans, dirty sneakers, and sloppy, oversize T-shirts. Suddenly every one of those girls seemed to be looking back at me. I felt awful, and it was all Mom's fault! She didn't know a thing about what Paxton girls wore!

Standing there, holding my lunch bag, I felt my face

growing warmer and warmer. Okay, I finally told myself, maybe I am an overdressed Texan, but that's not the worst thing in the world! Taking a deep breath, I pulled myself up tall and began walking toward the stage at the far end of the gym where a table had been set up. It was a long walk.

# CHAPTER 4

**Y**ou're full of school spirit today, aren't you!" said a smiling, gray-haired woman in a Paxton sweatshirt. She was standing behind the clinic officials' table.

"Yes, ma'am," I told her, digging my permission slip out of my lunch bag.

She took the paper from me. "Oh, so *you're* the one from Texas." Her blue eyes twinkled. "Hi, Patti. I'm Mrs. Holland, the cheerleading sponsor. I've had a few conversations with your mother. She likes to get all the details straight, doesn't she?"

"Yes, ma'am." I smiled back at her. "She sure does."

"Come on," Mrs. Holland said. "I'll find you some company."

I hurried across the gym after her to where half a dozen girls sat on the floor, stretching and talking.

"Girls, this is Patti Richardson," Mrs. Holland said to them. "She's just moved here from Dallas."

"Hi," a few of them mumbled weakly.

"They'll take good care you, Patti." Mrs. Holland

smiled again. "Here, give me your lunch and I'll put it in the refrigerator."

"Thank you, ma'am," I said, handing her the bag.

As soon as Mrs. Holland was out of earshot, a dark-haired girl wearing violet lipstick burst out laughing. "Thank you, *ma'am*?" she squealed.

At that the rest of the girls in the group began giggling. A pang of homesickness hit me so hard it almost knocked me down.

Then someone behind me said, "That is one fantastic outfit!"

I whirled and saw a tall, pale girl with thick brown bangs and blue eyes. Was she making fun of me, too?

"Oh, you like it, *ma'am?*" the violet-lipstick girl said.

"Yes, *ma'am,* I do." The tall girl mimicked the violet-lipstick girl's voice perfectly. "Come on," she said to me. "The other side of the gym isn't infested with rats."

Close to tears, I followed her. Instead of cutoff jeans and a sloppy T-shirt, the girl I was walking behind had on a brilliant yellow tank top and royal blue spandex bike pants. Her socks were blue too, and she wore black-and-white zebra-print sneakers. By the time we'd reached the other side of the room, I'd calmed down a bit.

"We're the only ones who showed up in the school colors," the girl said as we sat down on the gym floor and started stretching. "We ought to get some points just for that." She grinned. "I'm Tara Miller."

"I'm Patti Richardson," I said. "Thanks for . . . you know."

"No sweat." Then, faking an English accent, she

22

added, "You probably had no idea that you were in the presence of royalty."

"Royalty? That girl with the purple lipstick?"

"Right. Darcy Lewis—the Queen of Mean. Oh, hey! There's Amy!" Tara waved to a girl across the room, and then turned to me and confided, "No one can believe I'm here for this clinic."

"Why?"

"I'm not the cheerleader type." Tara shrugged. "I'm doing it for the experience. You know, so I can draw on it later, in my acting career."

Grateful as I was to Tara for rescuing me, I started to worry. Nobody in Texas talked that way about cheerleading!

"Are you?" Tara asked.

"Am I what?"

"The cheerleader type."

I nodded. "I've been a cheerleader practically all my life."

"Great! Maybe you can show me a few moves." Tara broke into another grin. "Where are you from, anyway?"

"Texas," I told her. "Dallas."

"Wow," said Tara. "I bet it'll be different for you here."

I nodded again. "It already is."

Mrs. Holland announced that we should take seats then, so Tara and I moved closer to the stage and sat down on the floor along with about fifty other girls. On the stage the high school cheerleaders talked and laughed with the girls on the junior high squad. If I made

23

the squad, I'd be wearing the uniform they had on: a blue pleated skirt and a white sleeveless top with a big yellow P across the front.

"Welcome to the seventh-grade cheerleading clinic," said Mrs. Holland. "We'll begin today with a demonstration of everything you'll need to know for tryouts—required and optional jumps, the required cheer, partner stunts, and spotting. After that the cheerleaders will go around the room and pick groups of four to work with, and after lunch you'll make up an original group cheer." Mrs. Holland smiled. "We think this gets right to the heart of cheerleading, which, after all, is teamwork.

"Now," Mrs. Holland added, "since our squad coach, Beth Ann Sorel, is out of town, I'll turn the program over to the captain of the Paxton High cheerleaders, Salleen Cook."

A girl with light brown skin and dozens of slender braids with little beads on the ends stepped to the front of the stage.

"I'm happy to see so many of you here today," said Salleen. "Stunts are risky. Every girl on our squad has sprained an ankle or pulled a ligament, but so far we haven't had a serious injury, and I think it's because Beth Ann showed us how to break our stunts down into small steps and practice each step until we get it right. *Then* we put the steps together and do the stunt. It takes longer this way," Salleen went on, "but when we've mastered a stunt, we're really sure of it, and out there on the field we are super steady."

Salleen turned toward the other members of the high school squad. "Okay, people, let's raise some spirit!"

The cheerleaders lined up.

I sat up on my heels to get a better view. In seconds I'd know whether what I called cheerleading was what Paxton called cheerleading. I held my breath and waited.

Salleen called: "Ready, and!"

As the squad went into action, I started breathing again.

> *Hey . . . you! Out in the crowd!*
> *If you've got spirit, clap out loud!*

They'd done a cheer I knew—and knew *well!* Their arm motions were more military style than the ones I was used to, but they were nothing I couldn't pick up. Best of all, the jumps looked just like the jumps back home!

After the cheer everyone started clapping, and I felt such relief spread over me that before I thought about it, I popped up onto my knees and started circling my right arm in the air over my head and *yaaaa-hoooing* the way we used to do for the Belton Bulls. Suddenly I realized I was *yaaaa-hoooing* alone.

But just as I felt my face getting all hot again, Tara jumped up and began circling her arm in the air. She let out an earsplitting *yaaaa-hooo* worthy of any Texan.

Then the cheerleaders picked up the arm circling and started *yaaaa-hoooing* too. Before long all the kids at the clinic were on their feet. It took a *long* time for all the *yaaaa-hoooing* to quiet down, and by the time it did, I didn't feel like such a stranger anymore.

# CHAPTER 5

"I want the girls dressed in the school colors in my group!" Salleen called as she made a beeline for Tara and me after the demonstrations were over.

"All right, Captain Salleen!" said Tara, saluting. "Tara Miller, reporting for duty."

Salleen laughed, and then turned to me.

"I'm Patti Richardson," I said, mentally apologizing to Mom for ever doubting her cheerleading savvy.

"Where'd you learn to whoop like that?" Salleen asked, and I found myself telling her about my cheerleading in Texas.

"I can't wait to see your stuff," she said. "Listen—"

"Salleen!" called a small, dark-skinned girl as she dashed across the gym. Her hair was pulled back in a bun with wispy bangs in the front. She had on an oversize purple T-shirt with white letters that said GYMNASTS ARE WELL BALANCED.

"Hey, Lauren!" Salleen cried as the girl ran into her arms and the two of them hugged. "I was looking for you before."

26

"Mom had an emergency," Lauren said, panting hard, "and she went to the hospital, so I had to get here on my bike."

Now *that's* dedication! I thought. Her mom had some kind of horrible emergency—bad enough to put her in the hospital—and Lauren still came to the clinic!

"Find a partner," Salleen told her, "and be in my group."

Lauren looked around. "Tara!" she exclaimed suddenly. *"You?* At a cheerleading clinic?"

"See?" Tara elbowed me. "I told you I wasn't the cheerleader type." She smiled. "Patti, meet Lauren, who, like myself, is a graduate of Paxton Elementary in beautiful downtown Paxton."

"Lauren!" two PJHS cheerleaders called.

Lauren turned. "Andrea! Christina!" she called back, and waved. Then she grabbed Tara's arm and the two of them ran over to talk with the girls, who I guessed had gone to their old school too.

As they ran off, a tiny girl with curly red hair in a side ponytail came up to where Salleen and I were standing. A pair of yellow earphones rested around her neck, and she had a black canvas backpack slung over one shoulder. Her lavender V-neck shirt looked really pretty with her red hair.

"I'd like to join your group, please," she told Salleen.

Salleen looked at the girl with the serious brown eyes as if trying to place her. "Do I know you?" she finally asked.

"No, you don't," answered the girl. "I'm Cassie Copeland."

27

Cassie's bright yellow tape player was hooked to a beaded belt that went through the loops of a pair of dark green jeans—jeans that I knew, from flipping through fashion magazines on the trip north, were the very latest color.

"Sure, you can be in my group," said Salleen. "You look just the right size to be a flier in stunts."

"I suppose so," said Cassie. "I've never actually done any cheerleading before."

"Hey, me neither!" Tara announced happily as she and Lauren returned to Salleen's side.

"Two beginners, hmmm?" said Salleen. "We can fix that. But Cassie, how come you're so interested in being in my group?"

"Because you're the captain," Cassie said matter-of-factly. "If I become a cheerleader, I'd definitely plan to be captain of my squad."

"Well, that's up front!" Salleen laughed. "Lauren, you and Patti can partner the girls who are new at this, okay?"

I nodded and looked over at Lauren. I wondered if she was worried about her mother being in the hospital.

"Okay, you're a team now." Salleen put a hand out toward us, her palm facing down. We all stacked one hand and then the other on top—Cassie, then Lauren, then Tara, then me. "You're going to work superhard," Salleen said, "and by Friday, I'm going to see four girls who are ready to be Paxton cheerleaders!"

She lowered her hand and popped it up, sending all our hands into the air. The five of us *yaaaa-hoooed* up a storm.

\*     \*     \*

When lunch was announced, there was a mad rush for the refrigerator. The four of us found our lunches and sat on the floor together under a big PAXTON RULES! banner.

I felt shy about taking my sandwich out of the bag. I didn't want to stick out as different again. Tara was eating a tuna sandwich, chips, and a Coke. Lauren had opened a container of fruit salad and was spearing purple grapes and cantaloupe wedges with a plastic fork. Cassie's whole-grain bread looked as if it held nothing but lettuce and sprouts. There didn't seem to be one-and-only-one cool thing to eat for lunch here in Paxton, so I guessed it was safe to pull out my turkey sandwich.

"Where'd you go to school last year?" Tara asked Cassie.

"Paxton Heights," Cassie said.

"Oh, la-de-da," said Tara.

Cassie looked annoyed. "What's that supposed to mean?"

"You know," said Tara. "Ritzola. Big houses. The works."

"That may be true," Cassie said, "but so what?" She turned to Lauren. "Have you been cheering long?" she asked.

Lauren shook her head. "This is my first time trying out. I've practiced a lot, though. Salleen's been coaching me. My big brother, Jed, and Salleen are, like, in *love*." Lauren giggled. "They've been going out for over a year, and they'd better not break up—at least not while Salleen's my coach!"

29

Cassie looked thoughtful. "I could use some individual coaching. Do you think Salleen would work with me?"

"Probably," said Lauren. "Ask her."

"Maybe she'd trade cheering lessons for voice lessons with my mother," Cassie said. "I was reading last night that sometimes cheerleaders study with voice teachers to learn to project their voices and to pronounce words clearly."

Lauren laughed. "What kind of books have you been reading?"

Cassie's face reddened a little. "Well," she admitted, "when I decided to try out for cheerleading, I did read up on the subject." She dug around in her big backpack and pulled out three books on cheering. "I like to be thorough."

"Your mom teaches singing?" Tara asked Cassie. "I've always wanted to take voice lessons."

"Mother studied to be an opera singer," Cassie said, "but it never happened." Frowning, she seemed lost in her own thoughts.

"Salleen's been trying to help me get my voice lower and louder," Lauren told us. "But nothing seems to work." She shrugged. "I do okay on the stunts because I used to be into gymnastics."

"*Into* gymnastics?" Tara turned to Cassie and me. "It was a little more than that. Lauren took first place in her age group at the Indiana State Championships last year. Everybody at our school thought she was on her way to the Olympics."

"Really?" Cassie's eyes widened. "And you *quit?*"

"Yep," said Lauren. "My best friend, Danielle, and

30

I went to the nationals, and we met girls who practiced gymnastics twelve hours a day. They didn't go to school—they had private tutors. Some of them even moved away from home to live with their coaches. Their whole lives were gymnastics." She shook her head. "Danielle couldn't wait to get more serious about gymnastics, but I just didn't picture my life that way."

"I know what you mean," Cassie said. "When I studied ballet, all the girls in my class could talk about was leotards and toe shoes and whether they looked fat. They lived for ballet." She frowned again, then added, "Mother wasn't too happy when I quit."

"My parents weren't too thrilled either," admitted Lauren. "But last fall I went to a football game with my cousin Corva, who's a cheerleader at Delmar High, and for the first time I tuned in on the way the cheerleaders worked together as a team. I decided that I'd rather do flips at a football game than on the balance beam." She smiled. "Convincing my parents to let me switch to cheering wasn't that easy. They thought I had a shot at the Olympic team and I should go for it. Especially my mom."

"Speaking of your mom," I said, "you think she'll be okay?"

Lauren looked at me strangely. "Sure," she said. "I mean, my quitting gymnastics wasn't *that* big a deal to her."

"I meant," I said quickly, "that when you got here you said your mom had to go to the hospital, that it was an emergency."

31

Lauren started laughing. "It was—but not my mom's. She's an obstetrician, and she had to deliver a baby."

"Oops," I said, laughing with her.

"Lauren's dad is a doctor, too," Tara told me.

Lauren nodded. "A pediatrician. And guess what my parents want their four kids to be when we grow up?"

But before we could all guess *doctors,* two more girls ran up, shrieking, "Lauren!" They hugged her. She sure seemed to have a lot of friends.

Lauren introduced Cassie and me. The girl with a million freckles was Liz, and the one with short blond hair and sort of crooked teeth was Michelle.

"Tara!" exclaimed Liz. "I can't believe you're here!"

"Believe it, woman," said Tara.

"Hi, Patti," said Michelle, and she began circling her arm in the air. Just as I started thinking that she was making fun of me, she added, "You were great!"

"She ought to be great," said Tara. "Patti's been a cheerleader since birth."

"Patti," Cassie said as Liz and Michelle left, "since you have the most experience, can you tell us what might give us an edge over the competition? Any tips?"

My mind drew an absolute *blank.*

"In Texas," I said at last, "spirit was pretty important."

"Spirit?" said Cassie. "What *is* spirit, exactly?"

"You know." I looked helplessly at Lauren. "School spirit. Smiling is definitely the number-one thing that judges use to rate spirit. Smiling, and having lots of energy and pep."

"Cassie, what are you doing?" Tara demanded.

What Cassie was doing, I realized, was writing down everything I said in a small, spiral-bound notebook. "I'm just getting the facts," she said. "Go on, Patti."

I tried to think. "Well, eye contact is important. My mom's always telling me to look the judges in the eye."

"Your *mom?*" said Tara. "What is she, your coach?"

And so I explained about Mom and Aunt Peggy and everything. When I finished, I said, "Now I have a question. When the kids here vote for cheerleader, do they—"

"Hold it," demanded Tara. "How do kids in Texas vote on cheerleaders?"

"Well," I said, "at the school I would've gone to if we hadn't moved, judges pick twenty-four girls at try-outs, and they cheer at this huge pep assembly and then the whole school votes for twelve girls."

Lauren gasped. "That's awful!"

"It's ridiculous," Cassie added. "Cheerleading today is a team sport, like soccer or basketball. When kids try out for a sport, the coaches pick the best players. No one votes on them."

"Does that mean"—I looked from Tara to Cassie to Lauren—"that kids here *don't* vote for the cheerleaders?"

"No way," said Tara. "Here in Paxton, you have to make it on your talent alone."

I felt a smile spread across my face. "I can't believe it!" I cried. "That's the best news I've had in a long time!"

Tara laughed. "Because you're so incredibly talented?"

"No!" I said quickly, feeling my face getting warm again. "I just didn't think kids would, you know, vote for a new girl."

"But Pah-ti!" Tara said in a funny Dracula voice. "You are *not* joost any new girl. You have cheerleadink in your *blood!*"

34

# CHAPTER 6

*H*elp!" cried Tara. "My arms are falling off!"

"Now you're getting the T-motion!" Salleen exclaimed.

Salleen was teaching us to make fists and then fling our arms straight out to the side so that our bodies formed the letter *T*. Sounds easy, right? Try it for an hour or so sometime.

In Texas when we did hand motions, we didn't make fists. We held our hands in what we called "blades," with our fingers closed and our hands cupped slightly.

We'd practiced arm motions for what seemed like hours when Mrs. Holland announced: "Take a break, girls!"

A great rock song by Mad Scientist began blaring out over a loudspeaker. Right away Tara and Lauren started doing a line dance. They were both great—especially Tara, which surprised me a little. Tara wasn't limber, and she had trouble doing crisp arm motions. But when it came to funky dance moves, she knew what she was doing. I stood behind her and tried to pick up the steps.

Looking over, I saw Cassie with her earphones on, just standing there, watching. After a few minutes I danced over to her. "It's not that hard!" I shouted over the music.

"Oh, I know." Cassie clicked off her tape player and took off her earphones. "This just isn't my kind of music. When Mother convinced me to come here today, she never mentioned anything about rock."

"Your mom *made* you come here today?" I asked.

Cassie nodded as the song ended. "She said the teamwork aspect of cheerleading might help my interpersonal skills."

"Your *what?*" I was beginning to think that people here in Paxton sure had some strange attitudes about cheerleading!

The next song started blasting. I grabbed Cassie's arm. "Come on!" I pulled her over to Tara and Lauren. "We're a team, remember? It doesn't feel right dancing without you."

Cassie and I positioned ourselves behind Tara and Lauren and started dancing. Again I was surprised—Cassie could really *move!* By the time the song was over, she'd leaped to the front of the line and was leading the rest of us.

As we stood there catching our breath, I said, "Wasn't that more fun than listening to your classical music?"

"What makes you think it was classical?" Cassie asked.

"I don't know—I guess because you said your mom studied to be an opera singer and all."

Cassie smiled. "My mother loves classical," she admitted. "My father, too. He hosts a classical music radio show, 'Mozart in the Morning.' "

"My gram loves that program!" Lauren exclaimed. "That's your *dad?* With the really deep voice?"

Cassie nodded. "That's him. 'The Classical Music Monarch.' But," she added quickly, "I have my own taste."

As she said that Cassie whipped her earphones from around her neck and handed them to me.

I put them to my ears, pressed *play,* and listened. "I don't believe it!" I exclaimed, pulling off the earphones. *"Country?"*

Cassie smiled. "I started listening to it just to rebel against my parents' taste. They think country music is even *worse* than rock. But then it grew on me, and now I really like it."

"Me too!" I cried, and we started talking a mile a minute about our favorite singers and songs.

"I hate to break up this conversation," said Salleen as she hurried over to us, "but it's time to stretch out those legs."

Lauren and I hit the floor and brought our legs straight out to the sides of our bodies. Cassie's *V* was wide too. But Tara had trouble. She had even more trouble when Salleen asked us to slowly bend over, bringing our chins to our knees.

Salleen squatted beside Tara. "Don't bounce," she said. "Find the place where you're stretched to your limit and then just breathe into it."

Tara tried. From where I was, I could hear her breathing into her stretch. Groaning was more like it. But she

37

wasn't making much progress. At last she jumped up and started strutting around us, chanting:

*Sit on your backside, stretch your legs out wide!*
*Put your chin on your shin! Put your nose on your toes!*
*Stretch it out! Stretch it out! Hey! Hey!*

"Tara! You're not taking this seriously!" Cassie scolded.

But Tara looked so funny that Lauren and I started laughing and collapsed out of our stretches. Salleen cracked up too.

"Where'd you learn such a crazy cheer?" Salleen asked.

Tara made a face. "It's an original Tara Miller."

"Hey, great!" Salleen cried. "You've just volunteered to make up the group cheer." Salleen looked at us. "Right, people?"

"Right!" said Cassie. "Here—" She dug around in her backpack. From her notebook she pulled several large note cards and a pen. "You might as well get started on it now."

Smiling, Tara took the writing supplies. "Making up a cheer sure beats stretching," she said, and she went off by herself to compose.

The rest of the afternoon flew by. It didn't take me long to figure out that *unlearning* my old habits was going to be a lot harder than learning new moves.

We worked on our original group cheer, but by the time we figured out which arm motions, jumps, and other stunts went with which words, it was nearly three o'clock.

"That's it for today, people," said Salleen. "You'll have to finish your group cheer tomorrow."

Even with all my weeks of practicing, I knew my muscles were going to be sore that night. I was ready to go home.

"Just a minute," Cassie called out as everyone started to leave. "I think we should do the group handshake again."

She stretched her hand out the way Salleen had done earlier, palm down. One by one we put our hands on top of hers.

"We're a team," Cassie said.

"What a team!" added Lauren.

"Is the team in serious pain?" asked Tara. "Or just me?"

"We're all in this together," I said, and Cassie popped our hands up.

A wonderful feeling came over me then. This morning I'd been a stranger. Now I was part of a team. The four of us *had* to make cheerleader together. We just had to! Right then I made a vow. Not a vow of silence, but one of teamwork. I promised I'd do whatever it took to keep our team together.

That night, after dinner and a quick call to Melody, I dumped a double dose of Soothing Bath Crystals into the tub. Two minutes later I was soaking under six inches of bubbles with just my head sticking out. Ah . . . My body relaxed while all the events of the day spun around in my head.

I couldn't believe Darcy Lewis had made fun of me! What a creep. But at least kids didn't vote for cheerleader here. That was a *big* plus. And so was Tara Miller. She'd saved me from the two most awful, embarrassing moments of my life. She'd even promised to point out things I said that sounded "too Texas" so I wouldn't get teased again. Even though I'd only known her for a day, Tara was already a good friend.

But I was worried about her. She was a terrific dancer and made up really great cheers, but Tara's jump had a long way to go. I'd checked out the other girls at the clinic, and lots of them could do a pretty good toe-touch jump. Without some serious coaching and without a toe-touch jump, Tara didn't have a chance of making the squad. But what if, I thought, what if . . .

"Patti?" Mom opened the door a crack. "May I come in?"

"Sure," I said. At dinner I'd told my family everything I could think of about the clinic, but I knew Mom was here for more.

She lowered the toilet lid and sat down. "Now tell me truthfully, honey, you think you'll make the squad?"

"I don't know, Mom. The hand motions they do here aren't that different, but I get mixed up, and it makes me look sloppy."

Mom nodded. "Practice should take care of that."

I wiggled my toes under the bubbles and decided to ask what I'd been thinking about. "Mom? You know the girls in my group? I really want us all to make the squad. Together."

"That's the team spirit!" Mom beamed me her supersmile.

"And," I went on, "I was thinking, when clinic ends on Friday, could everybody come here for a sleepover?"

"Why, Patti, that's a wonderful idea!"

"I mean, maybe they won't be able to come, but if they did, we could practice together." I smiled up at Mom. "And maybe you could watch us and help us with what we're doing wrong?"

Mom's hundred-watt smile brightened to five-hundred watts. "I'll coach you all in the cartwheel room!" she exclaimed. "It'll be just perfect!" She jumped up, planted a kiss on my forehead, and then left me to my bubbles.

Mom could be a little much sometimes, I thought. But when it came to cheerleading, that's *exactly* what Tara needed.

# CHAPTER
## 7

**W**here's Tara?" Cassie asked the next morning. "It's almost nine thirty. It's not good to have a team member who's late."

Cassie, Lauren, and I were down on the gym floor, stretching. After the reaction to my outfit the day before, I wasn't taking any chances. I'd left my hat at home and wore a pair of cutoffs and a plain white T-shirt. Lauren had on cutoffs too and another oversize T-shirt, and Cassie was wearing a soft gray summer-weight sweatshirt and sweatpants.

I was nervous about inviting everyone to my house. What if they didn't even call them sleepovers here? Would they think it was babyish if I asked them to bring sleeping bags? I needed Tara to be there when I did the asking.

Cassie glanced at her watch. "I hope lateness isn't a habit with her."

"What's a habit with who?" Tara said as she walked over to our group. She was wearing the school colors again, only today her bike pants were bright yellow and her tank top was royal blue. From one earlobe dangled a large yellow feather. From the other, a little blue plastic megaphone.

"Being late," answered Cassie. "Why are you late, anyway?"

Tara shrugged. "My mom had to get up for an early haircut client, and she forgot to reset her alarm for me."

"Maybe you should get your own alarm," Cassie suggested.

"Maybe you should mind your own business," snapped Tara.

"You're in my group, so it *is* my business," said Cassie.

"Oh, don't have a cow." Tara looked annoyed. "Anyway, it doesn't look like I missed much. Salleen's not even here."

"She's talking to Mrs. Holland," Cassie explained. "We're supposed to stretch until she gets back." She bent over her left leg. "I hope you remembered to bring the group cheer."

"Oh, no!" Tara put her hands to her face, looking horrified.

Cassie straightened up. "I don't believe it!" she cried.

"Just kidding!" Tara grinned and plopped down beside me. She began stretching halfheartedly.

"Great earrings," I whispered, bending over my left leg.

"You like them?" She wiggled a finger under the feather. "They're from Trinkets, this little boutique in Chicago."

"Cool," I said. "Do you go into Chicago much?"

"At least once a month. My parents are divorced, and my dad lives there. When I visit him, my stepmother, Diane, always takes me to Trinkets to check out the earrings." She waved to someone across the room and then added, "This summer, I started taking the train in by myself. I love going, and I've got the cutest little stepsister, baby Lucy."

"I love going to Chicago too," Lauren said. "The clothes shopping is much better than at the Paxton Mall."

Cassie checked her watch. "I think we should move on to practicing the arm motions we learned yesterday," she said.

"Wait a second," I said before everyone could stand up. "I wanted to ask you all if . . . after clinic's over tomorrow . . . would you all like to come to my house for a sleepover?"

"That sounds great," said Tara.

"Yeah," chimed in Lauren. "That way we can keep practicing."

My nervousness disappeared. "We have this room in our house with mirrors that's perfect for cheering practice, and my mom said that if we want her to, she'll help us."

"Individual coaching is just what I need," Cassie said. "I'd love to come."

"Fantastic!" I cried. "Oh, and could you all give me your phone numbers? Mom wants to call your parents tonight and, you know, make the invitation official."

"You're kidding," said Tara.

I looked at her blankly. "Well, no," I said.

"Your mom doesn't have to waste her time calling my mom." Tara shook her head. "I mean, I handle my own social life."

"But we just moved here and all," I tried to explain, "and my mom thought . . ."

"Here." Cassie pulled a note card from her notebook. She'd written her phone number on it. "My mother will *definitely* be home tonight," she said with an odd little laugh as she handed the card to Lauren.

Lauren wrote down her number and passed the card to Tara. Shaking her head again, Tara added her number and gave the card to me.

"Is your mom really willing to work with us?" asked Cassie.

"Willing?" I said. "She can hardly wait!"

"Should we bring sleeping bags?" Lauren asked.

"That's a great idea!" I gave a sigh of relief. "That way we can sleep in the cartwheel room."

"The *what?*" said Tara.

I laughed. "That's what we call the room with the mirrors. You'll see why when you get there."

Now Tara put out her hand, and we piled ours on top. "All for one and one for all," she declared.

"Like the Three Musketeers," said Lauren.

"Only we're the Four Musketeers," Cassie pointed out.

"No," I said. "We're the Four Muske*cheers!*"

As we popped up our hands everyone groaned, and I knew I'd inherited my dad's talent for telling truly awful jokes.

\*       \*       \*

That second day at clinic we worked twice as hard as the first. We stretched, then we practiced jump preparations—the little jumps you take before the big one—and then jumps. After lunch it was time for partner stunts.

"Since we've got two beginners," said Salleen, "we'll start with a simple pony sit." She motioned to Lauren. "You and I'll demonstrate." Then she motioned to me. "Patti, you can spot for us. Remember, people, for every flier, you must have a spotter."

I held out my hands. Salleen bent over, placing a hand on each knee. Standing behind her, Lauren counted to three and jumped onto Salleen's back, putting her arms out in a T-motion.

"Lauren's holding on by squeezing with her knees," Salleen explained. "Now we'll take this stunt up one degree."

Lauren counted again and popped up to a kneeling position on Salleen's back. She put her arms in the high-V.

"This is very basic," Salleen said as Lauren dropped back to the ground, "but it's a good steady stunt for tryouts."

"It really does look easy," remarked Cassie.

"I said basic, not easy," warned Salleen. "Okay, Patti, you be the base now and Cassie, you be the flier. I'll spot. Cassie, put your hands on Patti's back and jump up and down a few times to get the feel of it."

I placed my hands on my knees. Then without any warning Cassie leaped up onto my back! Instead of landing on my hips, she landed up by my shoulders. I lurched forward to keep my balance.

46

Cassie felt me totter. "Hold still!" she cried.

She squeezed with her knees—*hard*. Then she bent forward and threw her arms around my head!

"Mmmmpp!" I yelled, which was all I could yell with one of her arms hugged tightly across my mouth. Her other arm was wrapped over my eyes. I stumbled blindly forward and Cassie toppled sideways.

"Gotcha!" cried Salleen.

I straightened up, blinking.

"Are you girls okay?" Salleen asked.

"I'm okay," I said.

Cassie was quite pale. "How did that happen?"

"You got ahead of me," Salleen explained. "You were supposed to jump up and down, not jump on Patti."

"Sorry, Patti," Cassie murmured.

I could tell it had been hard for her to make a mistake, and it was even harder for her to apologize.

"Now," said Salleen, "let's try it again."

"Why don't Lauren and Patti try it?" Cassie suggested. "I'll watch."

"Hey, who's the coach here?" Salleen said. "You know when you fall off a horse, it's important to climb back on again, and it's the same in cheering. Otherwise you lose your nerve. We're going to keep this up until you do it *right.*"

And we did. It took three or four more wobbly tries before Cassie got the hang of the stunt. She started trusting me then, and I started trusting her. After a while Cassie felt almost as steady as Melody jumping onto my back.

Tara proved to be a good, sure base. She and Lauren

got their pony sit right away, so we moved on to the group cheer.

Tara had made a few word changes, and we all agreed the cheer was better than ever. Lauren and I quickly figured out which stunts we did best and Cassie put it all together.

"You know," Salleen said when we'd run through it a couple of times, "you four make a dynamite team!"

After practice I walked out to the van, slid open the door, and dove into the backseat.

"The bad news is that I have about twenty new bruises and my muscles are twice as stiff as they were yesterday," I moaned.

"What's the good news?" asked Missy.

"Everyone can come to the sleepover. They're bringing sleeping bags so we can sleep in the cartwheel room."

"That's just great, honey!" said Mom.

"Can I come to the sleepover too?" Missy asked.

I should have been ready for that question. But I wasn't.

"Well," I said, stalling for time, "to some of it."

"But not to all of it?" Missy sounded disappointed.

I sighed. I knew that the only friend Missy had made in Paxton so far was a big white dog named Spooky who lived next door. So I did feel sort of sorry for her. But on the other hand, I didn't know Lauren or Cassie or Tara very well. And I didn't want my little sister around when we were trying to have private conversations.

Suddenly I thought of the perfect solution. "Listen,

Missy, I told everyone that Mom would coach us. Would you help her?"

"Really?" said Missy, her eyes wide. She glanced over at Mom. "Can I, Mom? Can I help you coach the big girls?"

"Sure you can, Missy." Mom gave me a grateful look in the rearview mirror.

I leaned back in my seat. That took care of Missy at the sleepover—at least I hoped it did. Now all I had to do to was ask Mom and Dad not to get too mushy in front of everyone and make Dad promise not to tell any of his horrible old jokes.

# CHAPTER
# 8

**W**e're having a mock tryout!" Lauren exclaimed, running up to me as I walked into clinic on Friday morning.

"When?" I asked. "Now?"

Lauren nodded. "It's a surprise. Mrs. Holland just made the announcement. Come on!" She grabbed my arm and started pulling me over to the bleachers. "We all have to be sitting together before our group can get a number card."

The bleachers were filled with bunches of girls, huddled together, talking excitedly. Cassie sat by herself midway up the bleachers, looking very grouchy.

One of the PJHS cheerleaders called up to her, "Is everyone in your group here yet?"

"Not yet," Cassie called back down.

Tara was late again.

By the time she arrived, the cheerleader handed us the one-and-only card she had left: number thirteen.

"We're *last!*" Cassie hissed at Tara. "The worst position!"

"Sorry, guys." Tara took a seat beside me on the bleachers and stared at her zebra-print sneakers.

"Attention, girls!" When we quieted down, Mrs. Holland explained how the mock tryouts would work. Each group would start with a "spirit run," which is a way of running and cheering at the same time so that a crowd gets all excited. Then we'd do individual cheers. Finally we'd get the words to a short cheer, and each group would have ten minutes to make up motions and jumps to go with it. The judges would mark score sheets, and we'd get to see our scores. Mrs. Holland finished by saying, "Now let's see your school spirit!"

"Group one," Salleen called, "assume the on-deck position."

As the group jogged over to the corner of the room Cassie held out her hand. "Remember, we're a team!"

When Salleen wasn't around, Cassie just naturally took charge. I put my hand on hers and then Lauren added hers. Tara paused for a second, eyeing Cassie, before slapping her hand on top, saying, "Here's to saving the best for *last!*"

"Now performing," called Salleen, "group one."

Four girls ran out from the corner of the gym, shouting and doing cartwheels. We whooped and hollered for them. They were pretty good. Tara and Lauren told me that two of the girls had been on the Paxton Elementary squad last year. Still, I thought our group was better. The same with group two, group three, and group four. But when group five ran out, it was a different story.

Tara nudged me. "It's your best friend, Patti."

"Yes, *ma'am,*" I said as I watched Darcy Lewis lead

her group in an amazing spirit run. They zigzagged all over the place, performing walkovers and handsprings.

"Those two on the left are definitely competition for us," Cassie remarked as she jotted down their routine in her notebook. "Who are they?"

"The tall one's Darcy Lewis," Tara said, "and her partner's Emily Greer." She pointed out a small girl with a brown ponytail. "The other two are Sarah Block and Zoe Kimmel."

Everyone in the bleachers cheered like crazy.

"What a jump," Lauren said as Darcy did her cheer.

"A killer," agreed Tara. "But Darcy didn't make the Paxton Elementary squad last year. Neither did Emily."

"How come?" I asked. "They're both so good."

"They are *now,*" Tara said, "because they went ballistic when they didn't make it and practically dedicated their lives to cheerleading. They went to some cheerleading camp this summer."

"Looks like it paid off," said Lauren.

The girls were getting into position for their group cheer.

"Ready, and!" yelled Darcy.

*We're ready! We're hot!*
*We'll make it to the top!*

As the group yelled the words *make it!* Zoe and Sarah slid into splits and Emily stepped up onto Darcy's leg, onto her back, then onto her shoulder. On the word

52

*top* she locked her knees in an awesome shoulder stand. Darcy and Emily looked like college cheerleaders!

Lots of girls were clapping and yelling, but Mrs. Holland stood up, an angry frown on her face. As Emily did her dismount, Mrs. Holland motioned group five over to her table.

"No spotters," whispered Lauren.

The room became very quiet. I heard Mrs. Holland say, "Judges are not impressed with risks. You could have been hurt."

Darcy put her hands on her hips. "Emily and I have been working on that shoulder stand all summer," she said. "We know *exactly* what we're doing. We don't need spotters cluttering things up."

Then Mrs. Holland made an announcement. "Girls, as we showed you on the first day of clinic, every flier must have an alert spotter in contact with the stunt. Group five failed to have a spotter, and in actual tryouts the group would be disqualified."

After that Salleen called group six, and we watched group after group perform. Some of the girls were pretty good. Lauren's friend Michelle did an amazing back walkover. But no group looked as good as group five.

At last Salleen called, "Group thirteen on deck." And off we went to the corner of the gym. While group twelve performed, we waited. I concentrated on not biting my nails.

Before I knew it, group twelve ran off the floor and Salleen announced: "Now performing, group thirteen."

With that Cassie led us in our spirit run. We whooped

and hollered, and ended it with a fast little break dance. The crowd cheered up a storm.

After the spirit run Cassie began her individual cheer. She looked fine. Then came Tara, who didn't look so fine. Her jump was awful, and worse, she made a goofy face and staggered around trying to be funny to cover her embarrassment. I could just imagine how the judges were scoring *that!* Lauren was next. Her hand motions were sharp, but in that big gym her voice sounded small and shrill. She had no problems, however, when she jumped up and did the splits in midair. The crowd went wild again.

"Patti Richardson!" I called when it was my turn. I was so nervous that my voice came out at half volume. I took a breath and started my cheer. Partway through it, I realized my hands weren't in fists—they were cupped, Texas style. Quickly I made fists, but thinking so hard about my hands made me forget about my arms. I got off the beat and made sloppy loops. What a mess! All I could do was put everything I had into my toe-touch jump. I bent my knees, did a little prep jump, and sprang up, stretching out my arms and kicking my legs up to my hands. I kept my head up, smiling at those judges. I landed the toe-touch and stood there with my arms in the air. It felt like my best jump ever.

Quickly we moved into formation for our group cheer. Cassie called: "Ready, *and!*"

*P-A-X! T-O-N!*
*Paxton! Paxton! That's the one!*

For each letter and word we did an arm motion. Then, with Lauren and Tara spotting, Cassie popped up into a perfect pony sit, holding up her first finger on the word *one!*

We waited a beat, then did the second part of the cheer. We repeated the arm motions, only this time we did them backward!

> *N-O-T! X-A-P!*
> *Even backward, you'll agree!*
> *Paxton spells out VICTORY!*

As we spelled out VICTORY, Cassie, Lauren, and I went wild doing *backward* handsprings and *back* walk-overs, while Tara just turned her *backside* toward the judges, gave a little wiggle, and raised her arms in a high-V.

We stood there catching our breath, listening to the crowd.

As the cheering died down, Mrs. Holland announced our lunch break. "Go get some fresh air," she told us. "Just stay on the school grounds and be back in here by two o'clock for your results."

Cassie, Tara, Lauren, and I hugged, and then we all started talking at once.

"My jump was a total disaster!" Tara wailed.

Cassie cried, "I kept pointing my toes!"

"My voice squeaked!" Lauren moaned.

"Nothing was as pitiful as my arm motions!" I cried.

But we all agreed that our group cheer had real pizzazz.

We walked back over to the bleachers then to get our things, and Cassie whipped out her notebook.

"Patti?" she said as she started jotting something down. "Do me a favor?"

"What?" I peeked over her shoulder and saw that she was listing the things we'd done right and wrong.

"I want to get my thoughts on this down before I forget them. Would you get my lunch when you go for yours?"

"Sure thing," I said.

*"Sure thang,"* Tara repeated in her version of a Texas twang.

"What?" I said. "Nobody here says 'sure thing'?"

Tara, Cassie, and Lauren all shook their heads.

"Okay," I said. "Then I don't either."

"And while you're at the refrigerator, Patti . . ." Tara began.

"Why don't I get everybody's lunch?" I finished for her, and then I took off.

While I was waiting in line, I felt a tap on my shoulder. I turned to face Darcy Lewis, purple lipstick and all.

"Nice jump," she said, cutting in front of me.

Why was she being friendly now? "Thanks," I managed. "You too. Your whole group was great."

"Well, Emily and I were, anyway. We spent the summer together at this incredible cheerleading camp." Darcy brushed a strand of hair out of her eyes. "Listen, after clinic is over, we're going to practice every day until tryouts. Do you want to practice with us?"

"But don't you already have four girls?" I asked.

She shrugged. "You're good enough to take Sarah's place."

"You mean you'd just . . ." I began.

"Dump her?" Darcy laughed. "Sure. She'd understand—it's nothing personal. Since Mrs. Holland thought up this group cheer thing, it's really important to try out with the best girls, and I just want the best."

I felt my face grow warm with anger. Would she really kick Sarah out of the group just because she'd seen someone better?

"Thanks anyway," I told her, "but I'm planning to practice with my group." At least I was now!

"That's a major mistake, Patti," Darcy advised as she reached the head of the line. "Listen, you have a great jump, but your arm motions stink. If you practiced with us, Emily and I could show you how to get them right, no problem."

"Move it, Darcy!" called a girl behind us in line.

Darcy acted as if she hadn't heard a thing.

"Really," she continued, "keep practicing with your group and you don't stand a chance of making the squad."

Darcy turned her back to me then and began pushing lunch bags around the top shelf of the refrigerator. She didn't seem to notice that when she slid out her plastic container, she knocked a bag to the floor.

"That better not be my lunch, Darcy!" the girl behind me called out.

Darcy simply stepped over the bag as she walked away.

The second she left, I picked up the lunch, put it back, and then dug around like crazy to find four brown bags. As I scrabbled for the lunches, Darcy's words echoed inside my head: *Keep practicing with your group and you don't stand a chance of making the squad.*

# CHAPTER
# 9

**H**ey! Check out the football players!" Tara pointed to the far end of the field. "Let's go ask if we can play!"

"You're kidding," Cassie said. "Aren't you?"

"My brother's probably over there right now." Lauren put her hand above her eyes to shield them from the sun. "Jed's coaching the seventh graders who are trying out for the team."

As we walked to the far end of the bleachers, I wished I could tell everybody about Darcy Lewis. But how could I, when she'd said that sticking with them was a big mistake!

Lauren straddled a bleacher bench and opened her lunch bag. "Oh, no!" she cried as she lifted out a bottle full of bright pink liquid. "I brought the wrong bag!"

"Yuck," said Tara. "That looks like the stuff my mom used to make me choke down when I got strep throat."

"It probably is," said Lauren. "It's antibiotics."

"Are you sick?" asked Cassie.

Lauren shook her head. "It's for my cat, Harpo. He's

got this upper-respiratory thing"—she put her hand to her own chest—"and I have to give this to him three times a day. Gram was supposed to give him the noon dose." She frowned.

"Maybe your dad's got some of that medicine around his office," Tara suggested.

"My dad doesn't exactly know about Harpo," Lauren confessed. "Neither does my mom. That's why I hid his medicine in a bag."

"You're kidding!" Cassie exclaimed.

"They said no more strays." Lauren was quiet, and then she brightened. "Jed's got the car. He'll take it home for me."

Lauren stuffed the medicine back into the bag and stood up. "Come with me, you guys," she said.

"Okay, but let's eat first," said Cassie as she handed Lauren half of her sprouty sandwich. I donated my carrot sticks and Tara threw in her chips.

A few minutes later the four of us crossed the field. "Jed!" Lauren called as soon as we were close enough.

A high school boy wearing a Chicago Cubs baseball cap turned around. He looked like Lauren, only he was twice her size.

"Hey, Laur. Hey, Tara." Jed turned to the three boys who were doing push-ups beside him and said, "Take a break, guys."

Lauren and Tara said, "Hi, Justin," to one of the boys as he stood up. He was almost as wide as he was tall. If I were carrying a football and saw Justin running to tackle me, I'd get rid of that ball fast! Jed introduced the other two boys. T.D. Yeager was tall with very blond hair, fair skin, and light blue eyes, and Drew Kelly was about my height. He had a round face, brown hair, brown eyes, and round glasses.

"Listen, Jed," said Lauren. "Do me a favor?" And she explained about Harpo's medicine.

"No way, Lauren!" Jed protested. "That stupid cat of yours isn't going to croak if he misses one dose."

"If he did," Tara pointed out, "it would be on your head."

Jed sighed and looked at his watch. "I guess I could take it on my lunch break. But you'll owe me, Laur— big time."

Lauren handed him the bag. "Just give it to Gram," she said.

While Lauren and Jed talked, Drew stared at me. "Um," he said at last, "did you just move into Berkshire?"

I nodded as my face grew warm. "How'd you know that?"

"I live there," Drew explained. "My mom kept trying to make me come over and meet you, but . . . you know." He made a funny face.

For a second nobody said anything. Then Drew went on, "Is your dad Wild Bill Richardson who played for the Cowboys?"

I nodded again, turning even redder.

"Wow," said Drew. "That's really awesome."

"Drew's a *major* football fan," Justin told us.

"Yeah," added T.D. "He's got the walls of his room plastered with pictures of every football player in the universe."

61

Drew socked T.D. in the arm for that.

"Okay, guys, back to work." Jed turned to Lauren. "Don't worry. I'll take the cat his stuff."

"Thanks, Jed," said Lauren. "See you."

Walking back across the field, Tara started asking me questions and I ended up telling practically my whole family history. "I'll show you all the scrapbooks tonight," I promised.

"Texas Patti says 'I'll show *y'all*,'" teased Tara.

"I will show you," I repeated, sounding like a robot.

Back in the gym Mrs. Holland handed out the score sheets, and the four of us knelt down on the floor to look at ours.

0 = POOR; 1 = FAIR; 2 = AVERAGE; 3 = GOOD; 4 = SUPERIOR

|  | #1<br>L.A | #2<br>C.C. | #3<br>T.M. | #4<br>P.R. |
|---|---|---|---|---|
| APPEARANCE:<br>(poise, dress, grooming) | 2 | 3 | 0 | 2 |
| VOICE:<br>(force, clarity) | 0 | 2 | 4 | 2 |
| JUMPS:<br>(height, spread, form) | 4 | 2 | 1 | 4 |
| CHEER MOTIONS:<br>(hand, arm, leg coordination) | 3 | 2 | 2 | 1 |
| GYMNASTICS:<br>(timing, form) | 4 | 2 | 1 | 4 |

GROUP SPIRIT RUN:     3
(leading crowd in cheering)

GROUP CHEER:     2
(smoothness, timing, originality)


"A zero in appearance!" Tara wailed. "I've got on Paxton's colors. What do they want?"

"Maybe something that would show you want to be part of a group instead of standing out so much," suggested Cassie.

"You didn't get a four, so don't lecture me!" huffed Tara.

I was shocked at my scores. I tried to calm down and think clearly. The two in appearance was because I had on cutoffs and a T-shirt. The two in voice was nerves. I knew that I could take care of those things before tryouts. But a one in hand motions! Could I learn to do them right by tryout time? I didn't know!

Salleen jogged past us then, and Tara called her over.

"A *zero* and two *ones?*" Tara shook her head. "I quit."

Salleen took the sheet from Cassie. "You got a four in voice, Tara," she said. "That's outstanding. And the two points you got for the group cheer were based *totally* on originality!"

Tara's smile returned. "It was a great cheer," she admitted.

"My scores are so . . . average," said Cassie glumly.

"How come I got a zero in voice?" Lauren said in a

high, squeaky tone. Then she let out a *loud,* frustrated roar.

Tara laughed. "I guess we can all improve. Even Patti got a one, and she's got cheerleadin-k in her blood!"

"What'd you pack in here, bricks?" Tara asked after clinic as she took a handle of Cassie's overnight bag and helped carry it outside, where Mom and Missy stood waiting by the van.

"Mom," I said, "this is Cassie, Lauren, and Tara."

"I am so happy to meet you girls!" Mom exclaimed loudly.

"And this is Missy," I added as my sister, suddenly shy, slid halfway behind Mom.

"Hey, Missy," said Tara, climbing into the back of the van. "I hear you're a dynamite cheerleader."

Missy beamed and scrambled into the back to sit beside Tara. My sister told Tara all about her Little League cheering, and Tara let her play with her megaphone earring. By the time we'd driven half a mile, Missy was Tara's number-one fan.

When Mom stopped at the Main Street light, Lauren pointed toward town. "I live right down this street," she said.

"Me too," said Tara. "It's just two blocks from here to the beautiful Lakeview apartment complex."

"You're not far from us, then," said Mom.

"I know," said Lauren. "I bike to Berkshire all the time." She turned to Cassie. "Where do you live?"

"Heights Hills," said Cassie.

"Wow! That hill is a killer," Lauren said. "I can never make it to the top without walking my bike. Can you?"

"I wouldn't know," Cassie said softly. "I don't own a bike."

We pulled into our driveway, and Missy and I helped everyone carry their things inside. Outside the cartwheel room I said, "Okay, drop your stuff," and I flung open the door.

Cassie, Tara, and Lauren ran in and gasped, just the way I'd done the first time. Then we all started turning cartwheels like crazy, and finally collapsed on the floor.

"This is *fantastic!*" Tara cried.

*"Go get 'em!"* called Petey.

"Who said that?" Cassie asked.

"Meet Petey," I said, and everyone crowded around his cage.

*"Get 'em!"* cried Petey. *"Kill 'em!"*

Lauren cracked up. "That reminds me," she said. "I'd like to phone Gram and check on Harpo."

We all went into the kitchen. While Lauren phoned, I poured iced tea. Mom made us a big plate of nachos. Then she asked Missy to help her with something, and the four of us went upstairs.

"Your room could be in a magazine!" Lauren exclaimed.

"You just love her *CATS* poster," Cassie scoffed.

Tara examined every picture on my bulletin board. "Nice baseball uniform, Patti. Who's this?"

"Melody," I said, feeling a stab of homesickness. "My best friend from Texas."

Then we sat around, snacking and talking. Tara talked

a lot about T.D. "Maybe T.D. and some other guys went over to Drew's house after practice," she suggested. "Let's walk around Berkshire and figure out where he lives."

"Let's not!" Cassie and Lauren and I cried together.

Tara started talking about boys I didn't know then, and my mind wandered back to Darcy Lewis. She *was* the Queen of Mean. All she cared about was making the squad—no matter whose feelings she stomped on. Tonight I planned to bring up the idea of us all practicing together until tryouts. I wished Darcy's awful words would stop running through my head: *Keep practicing with your group and you don't stand a chance of making the squad.*

After a while Mom peeked in at my door. "Are you all ready to show me some cheers?" she asked.

We ran down to the cartwheel room and got into formation.

"Wait for me!" cried Missy, running in. She'd changed into a pair of bike pants and a little sleeveless T-shirt. She looked like a small, blond version of Tara Miller.

"Fantastic outfit, Missy!" Tara said, obviously pleased.

"Can I cheer with you?" asked Missy.

"You're a coach!" I said. "Go over with Mom so you can see."

Cassie called: "Ready, *and!*"

## P-A-X! T-O-N!

When we finished, Mom yelled, "That was great, girls!"

66

"Great, girls!" echoed Missy.

"Mrs. Richardson? How did we look?" Cassie asked. "Patti said you could give us some advice on how we could improve."

"You girls want me to give you a few pointers?" asked Mom.

Cassie and Tara and Lauren all nodded and said, "Yes!"

They didn't have a clue what they were getting into.

For three solid hours Mom coached us. She never let us stop. She had us stretching, jumping, yelling our heads off. After all day at clinic, it was a little much.

"Hi, Sunny," Dad said, walking into the cartwheel room. He seemed sort of puzzled at seeing four girls lying on the floor. Missy had long since become bored with Mom's clinic and had gone off to play with Spooky.

"Bill! Is it seven o'clock already?" Mom looked at her watch in surprise. "My, how time flies when you're having a good time!"

Dad put his arms around Mom and gave her a big kiss.

Darn! I'd forgotten to ask my parents to cut the mushy stuff!

After the kiss finally ended, Dad said, "Sunny, sugar, these girls look as if they could use a little break and some dinner. Why don't I run down to Gino's and pick up a couple of pizzas?"

We all thought that was the best idea we'd heard all day.

# CHAPTER
## 10

"And here they are doing a herkie," I explained as we reached the last page of Mom and Aunt Peggy's scrapbook, showing the twins in a split jump with one leg forward and one back.

After polishing off two large pizzas, the four of us had come into the cartwheel room and sunk into the pillows with the scrapbooks.

"Incredible," said Tara, staring at the page.

Lauren nodded. "And look how the knees on their forward legs face straight up."

"You know," Cassie said as she started flipping through the pictures a second time, "your mom is a really demanding coach."

"Yeah," Tara agreed. "And I thought Salleen was tough."

"She was easy compared to Mrs. Richardson," said Lauren.

"When it comes to cheering," I said with a laugh, "my mom's sort of out of control."

"But she's wonderful," Cassie insisted. "If she'd help us practice from now until tryouts, we'd really improve." She turned to me. "You think your mother would let us come over here every day, Patti? You think she'd work with us?"

"Ooooh," moaned Tara. "Just the thought of that hurts!"

"It'd be like our own cheerleading camp," said Lauren.

I could hardly believe my ears. Just when I'd been about to suggest this very plan, Cassie beat me to it!

I ran and found Mom and dragged her into the cartwheel room so we could ask her. Of course she said yes. Her actual words were: "I think it's the *best* idea in the world! Let's start first thing Monday morning!"

"That gives us twelve days to practice," Cassie said, checking the calendar in her notebook.

If Tara worked—really worked—with Mom for twelve days, I thought, it might be enough to fix her jump.

Snapping her notebook shut, Cassie turned to my mom. "Mrs. Richardson? May I ask you a favor?"

"Sure thing," said Mom.

*Sure thing!* Tara and I glanced at each other and smiled.

"We just saw the pictures of you and your sister cheering," Cassie went on, "and I was wondering if you'd do a cheer for us."

"Oh, you all don't want to see a thirty-something-year-old woman make a complete fool of herself, do you now?" Even as Mom spoke, she was walking to the center of the room. She just couldn't help herself.

"Ready, *and!*" Mom began a University of Texas cheer, and I yelled right along with her. At the end she did a herkie, sprang into a front walkover, and slid into the splits.

Looking over at my three friends, I had to laugh. They all had the same wide-eyed, openmouthed expression on their faces.

"Boy, Mrs. Richardson," said Tara, "that was awesome."

We played a quick game of Clue with Missy before she went off to bed. (Mrs. Peacock killed Mr. Green with the rope in the Conservatory.) Then we changed into our pajamas and started making plans for our cheerleading camp on Monday.

"Let's start early," Cassie said. "How's eight o'clock?"

"Eight?" cried Tara. "No way!"

Cassie crossed her arms on her chest. "We have so much to work on, Tara. If you're not serious about this, don't come."

"I'm just not the early morning type," Tara complained.

"Nine would be better for me, too," Lauren added.

"Okay, we'll compromise," said Cassie. "Eight fifteen."

"Cassie!" cried Tara. "Get a life! It's summer vacation!"

"I have a life," Cassie said, "and part of my life includes making cheerleader. You saw those girls in group five. They're fantastic! If we want to beat them, we have to be even better!"

"But for me, that's impossible!" moaned Tara.

I could tell Lauren felt as bad as I did about Cassie and Tara fighting. But it was hard to figure out how to stop it.

"If that's your attitude," said Cassie, "then maybe you shouldn't practice with us. Maybe you shouldn't even try out."

"Don't say that, Cassie!" Lauren cried.

"No, Cassie's right," Tara said. "My bad attitude's bringing everybody down, so just consider me off the team."

"Tara!" I practically shouted. My mind was spinning, trying to find a way to stop this from happening. "Without you, there is no team."

"I agree," Lauren said softly. "Cassie, let me see our score sheet, please." Lauren studied it for a minute. "In gymnastics," she explained, "we'd analyze our scores to see where our problems were and what we could improve."

"Which for me would be everything," said Tara.

"Here goes," said Lauren. "The zero in appearance was partly your outfit."

"True," admitted Tara. "It wasn't exactly out of the cheerleader handbook."

"And you didn't handle it too well when you goofed up."

"You mean this?" Tara made the face she'd shown the judges.

"Right," said Lauren. "But you can fix those things, so appearance isn't a problem. Voice is definitely not a problem—at least not for you," Lauren added sort of sadly. "And with a little coaching, you'll get the arm motions."

"So that narrows my problems down to jumps and gymnastics," Tara said. "The two most important parts of cheerleading."

"That's where my mom comes in," I added quickly. "When she works with you, you get better fast."

"If," Tara said, "I can stand the pain." And then she got all dramatic. "And what, I ask you, is a little muscle pain compared to the heartbreak of not making the squad?"

We all cracked up at that—Cassie too. But even though I was laughing, deep inside I knew we hadn't quite solved our team problems. At least not yet.

"Okay," Cassie said, getting back to business. "How's eight thirty?"

"Perfect!" Tara fell back on her pillows. "Eight thirty's perfect!" Then she sat up. "Now let's forget about cheerleading for a while and have a MASH session."

"Great!" said Lauren. "Here's a pen and some paper."

"What's MASH?" I asked.

"It tells your future," said Tara mysteriously. "We'll do Lauren first so you can see how to play."

At the top of the paper Tara wrote big capital letters: M A S H. Down the page, under each letter, she wrote the name of a place to live: Mansion, Apartment, Shack, and House. Then she made categories: Boys, Cars, Numbers, Jobs, and Places. Lauren had to list five items for each category—five boys, five kinds of car, and so on. When she'd finished, Tara put the pen point on the paper. "Go," said Lauren. Tara closed her eyes and started drawing a spiral:

72

"Stop," said Lauren.

Tara stopped. She drew a straight line through the spiral and counted that it had passed through *four* lines.

Saying "one" on "Mansion," Tara began counting. When she got to "four" on "House," she crossed it out. "You're not going to live in a house," she announced. Tara kept counting. Every time she got to "four," she crossed out an item. Finally there was only one item left in each category, and Tara read Lauren's future.

"Lauren, you're going to live in a mansion and be married to Colby Williams . . ."

"Who's Colby Williams?" asked Cassie.

"He's on the Paxton football team," Lauren told her.

"And he's a total hunk," added Tara, "right, Lauren?"

"I guess." Lauren giggled.

"So you and Colby," Tara continued, "are going to drive a pickup truck and have five children."

"Not children!" Lauren corrected her. "Cats. Five cats."

"Okay," said Tara. "Your job is . . . parakeet trainer?"

"Petey inspired that one!" Lauren laughed.

"You're going to live," Tara finished up, "in the San Diego Zoo!"

"Lauren," said Cassie, "are you some kind of animal nut?"

"That's what my dad thinks," said Lauren. "My mom too."

"How come?" I asked.

"I seem to find strays." She shrugged. "Or maybe they find me because they know I'll give them a good home. When I was in third grade, I rescued a kitten from a garbage can in an alley—I named her Orphan Annie. Then," Lauren went on, "last summer I found a black-and-white tomcat outside the bakery and my sister named him Groucho, 'cause he's got this black mustache, and—"

"Wait," interrupted Cassie. "How many people are in your family?"

"Seven." Lauren started ticking them off on her fingers. "You met Jed, and there's Gary, who's six, and Amy, who's five, and me, and Mom and Dad and Gram, my mom's mother." Lauren smiled at Cassie. "How many in yours?"

"Just Mother and Father and me," Cassie said impatiently, "but I'm not finished asking you questions yet."

I knew Cassie didn't mean to be rude, but she sure sounded that way! Luckily Lauren didn't seem to notice.

"Now," Cassie went on, "how many cats do you have?"

"Three," said Lauren. "But Mom and Dad think we have two."

"You have other animals?" Cassie asked. "Besides cats?"

Lauren nodded. "Six gerbils—and more on the way— two guinea pigs, and a pair of lizards."

"I think you already live in a zoo!" Cassie shook her head. "My parents would never allow animals in our house."

"Awww," said Lauren sympathetically. "Not even a gerbil? I'm always looking for good homes for my babies."

"I've got two of Lauren's gerbils," said Tara. "Two females, Lily and Kirstie."

After that we did MASH on Tara, who ended up marrying T.D., driving a Porsche, and moving to Hollywood.

"It's perfect," said Tara. "Except for living in a shack."

We were too tired to MASH Cassie and me then. We spread out our sleeping bags on top of our tumbling mats. I turned off all the lights but one and turned up the radio for the midnight "Top Ten Countdown."

Before we snuggled down in our sleeping bags, Cassie said, "You know, Lauren, your voice doesn't project at all."

Honestly! Cassie did not know the meaning of tact.

"Yeah," Lauren said, "but I just don't know what to do."

"Why don't I ask Mother if she'll work with you?" Cassie suggested.

Lauren brightened. "Could she really help me?"

"She coaches singers to hit low notes all the time, so maybe she could," Cassie said. "I'll ask her and phone you tomorrow, but I think she will. For some reason

Mother's very supportive of anything connected with my cheerleading."

"You think she'd come over here Monday?" asked Lauren.

A funny look crossed Cassie's face then. "No," she said slowly. "You'll have to come over to our house."

"But if she came over here while we're having our cheering camp," I said, "maybe she could give us all a few pointers."

Cassie just shook her head.

"The Richardsons have a piano," Tara added.

"Mother cannot come over here," Cassie said firmly.

We all got very quiet then.

Cassie smiled nervously. "I guess I forgot to mention one little detail about Mother," she said at last. "She never goes out of our house."

# CHAPTER
# 11

"That'll be fifty cents, please," Missy said on Saturday night as the timer dinged, signaling the end of my ten-minute back rub. Lauren, Tara, Cassie, and I had put in a full day of practice in the cartwheel room, and I was feeling it.

"If your muscles still hurt," Missy told me, "you can have another five minutes for a quarter."

"Thanks anyway, Missy," I said, "but I'm broke."

The phone rang then and I picked it up.

"Patti? It's me, Lauren. Listen, Cassie just called. Her mother's asked me to come over tomorrow afternoon."

"That's great!"

"I guess. But ... it makes me nervous, going there alone."

"What do you think is the matter with Cassie's mother?"

"I asked my mom about it at dinner tonight," said Lauren, "and she said it might be agoraphobia...."

"What?"

77

"Agoraphobia," Lauren repeated slowly. "The *agora* was what the ancient Romans called their public market-place, and *phobia* means "fear of." Agoraphobia is a mental condition where people are afraid to go out into public places."

"Does your mom think Mrs. Copeland could be . . . dangerous?"

"No, not at all. My mom thinks I should go if I want Mrs. Copeland to help me, which I do. I just don't want to go alone."

I thought for a minute. "Maybe we should all go. You and me and Tara, too."

"Would you call Cassie and ask her if that's okay?"

"Sure." I hung up and phoned Cassie. At first she just kept saying that it wasn't necessary for all of us to come, but she gave in when I said, "We're a team, remember?"

"Let me check," Cassie said, and I held on. When she returned to the phone, she said, "Mother would be delighted if you and Tara came too. I have an idea— why don't we practice at your house from one to four and then come over here?"

Then I had to check. Naturally it was fine with Mom.

"Great," said Cassie. "Mother promised to help us all with voice projection, and then she'll serve tea."

"Thank your mom, Cassie!" I said. "I mean, your mother."

I phoned Lauren back and told her all the plans, and then I phoned Tara.

"Can you come over here at one to practice?" I asked her. "Then we're all going over to Cassie's to get some help with our voices." I told her what Lauren had said about agoraphobia, and finished by saying that Mrs. Copeland had said she'd serve tea.

"Tea at the Copelands'," said Tara. "La-de-da!"

"What's the big deal about tea?" I asked her. "In Texas everybody drinks iced tea all day long."

"Cassie's neighborhood is really fancy," Tara said, "and I bet Mrs. Copeland's tea will be fancy too."

When Cassie showed up at our house on Sunday, she was very quiet. I guessed that she was nervous about all of us coming over and meeting her mother. To tell the truth, I was nervous too!

We did a whole hour of cheerobics, which is cheering and aerobic dancing. When it came to dancing, Tara was the best. But when it came to jumping, it was a different story.

Cassie spent a long time showing Tara how to stretch her legs at the ballet barre, but it didn't seem to help her jump.

"I can't get off the ground!" Tara wailed.

After we worked on partner stunts, Cassie looked at her watch. "That's it for today," she said, and we ran up to my room to get dressed for the tea.

I jumped into the shower first while everyone else fussed with their outfits. When I returned to my room, it was wall-to-wall pants, T-shirts, socks, you name it, so I grabbed my clothes and went into Missy's room to change.

I put on my favorite summer dress. It had a white collar and tiny blue-and-white flowers printed all over it. Then I stepped into my white patent-leather flats. I undid my braid, and as I was brushing my hair Missy popped in.

"You look fancy," she told me.

"Thanks, Missy," I said. "Tara said the Copelands' house is really fancy, so I thought I'd be fancy too."

"You are," Missy assured me. "Lots fancier than the other girls."

I stopped brushing. "What do you mean, Missy?"

Without waiting for an answer, I ran to my room.

Tara was dressed in a light purple cotton top that came to just above her knees, deep purple leggings, and a pair of wild white sandals with straps that wound halfway up her legs.

"Patti," Tara said when she saw me, "what are you wearing?"

"I got this for my cousin's wedding last spring," I said.

"One of these days," said Cassie, who had on an emerald green cotton pullover and long black-and-green-print wide pants, "we have to take you shopping."

"You mean," I began, "that no one here wears ... dresses?"

"Sure they do," said Lauren, who wasn't wearing a dress herself but a denim shirt, a silver-and-turquoise belt, and an ankle-length white pleated skirt.

Looking at the three of them, I realized what they reminded me of—models from the pages of *Seventeen!* Suddenly, in my flowery dress, I felt like a seven-year-old.

"Maybe there's something I can change into," I said, heading for my closet but knowing that there wasn't.

"Never mind," Cassie said, grabbing my arm. "We

don't want to be late. That would make Mother most unhappy."

Thinking about meeting Cassie's mother drove all thoughts of clothes out of my mind. I was nervous enough as it was, and I certainly didn't want to meet Mrs. Copeland when she was unhappy!

As we ran down the stairs Dad whistled.

"Don't you girls look gorgeous!" Mom exclaimed. "You'd all get a four in appearance today!"

We piled into the van, and Mom took off.

As we drove down the hill Tara nudged me. "One of these days we have to find out where Drew lives," she whispered.

"Why?" I whispered back.

"You saw how he stared at you. Aren't you even curious?"

"No." But I did like the idea that he was a fan of my dad's.

Except for giving Mom directions, Cassie was pretty quiet on the drive. After about ten minutes we pulled into the circular driveway of a large gray stone house. It reminded me of a castle!

"Have a wonderful time!" Mom called after us as we followed Cassie up the walk. "I'll be back for you all at six."

Cassie opened the front door and we walked into a formal entryway, which had a pair of dark wooden benches that looked as if they'd once been in a church. None of us said a word.

"Well, you're right on time," said a short man with a deep voice as he hurried into the entry.

81

Cassie introduced us to her father. He was sort of bald in the front. What hair he had was turning gray. He wore thick, wire-rimmed glasses that magnified a pair of stern brown eyes.

Lauren said, "My grandmother listens to your show all the time, Mr. Copeland. She says you make her mornings beautiful."

Mr. Copeland's stern expression disappeared into a smile. "I appreciate the compliment, Lauren," he said. Then, turning to Cassie, he added, "Take your friends on back, Cassandra. Your mother is waiting for you in the conservatory."

*"Cassandra?"* I whispered to Tara as we followed Cassie down a marble-floored hallway.

"The *conservatory?"* Tara whispered back. "I thought that was only a room in Clue!"

Cassie's conservatory looked very much like the picture on the Clue game board. It had windows all around, like a greenhouse, and there were lots of plants. At the far end of the room stood a grand piano. I didn't even see the small, redheaded woman sitting on a dark wicker couch near the piano until she stood up to greet us. Her hair was piled loosely on top of her head, and she wore a long lavender dress. My first thought was that she looked exactly like an older, slightly taller Cassie. But as I walked closer I saw that her eyes were nothing like Cassie's lively brown ones. Mrs. Copeland had the saddest eyes I'd ever seen.

82

# CHAPTER
## 12

*W*elcome, girls," Mrs. Copeland said. Her voice was sweet and musical. "Come sit down for a while before we begin working."

"Mother," Cassie said, "I'd like you to meet Lauren Armstrong, Tara Miller, and Patti Richardson."

Just as Mr. Copeland had done, Cassie's mother reached out to shake our hands. Her hand felt very delicate and cold as ice.

"Hello, Patti," she greeted me. "What a lovely dress you're wearing. It suits this room, I think."

Mrs. Copeland seemed like the last mother in the world to ever *make* her daughter go to a cheerleading clinic. She gazed at us now with a sort of sad smile and said, "Cassandra tells me that voice projection is very important in cheerleading."

No one said anything, so I piped up. "Yes, ma'am. In Texas, where I come from, we tried to get our voices loud and low."

Mrs. Copeland nodded. "That would be best for your

vocal cords. I wonder if, before we do some exercises, each of you would tell me why you want to become a cheerleader."

"What I like best," I told her, "is getting everybody at a game all excited so they'll cheer like crazy for their team."

"I like cheerleading," said Lauren, "because it takes teamwork." She smiled over at Cassie.

"For me it's definitely performing," said Tara. "Someday I want to be an actor," she added.

As each of us gave our answers, Mrs. Copeland nodded as if she were listening hard to every word. When we'd finished, she said, "Thank you. That was most interesting." Then she stood up. "Will you stand, please?" We did. "Now, keep your chests lifted and we will start with some breathing exercises."

And so our voice projection workshop began. After we breathed for a while, Mrs. Copeland asked us to imagine that we had a string pulling up on our breastbones.

As we tried to get our voices deeper and deeper, I thought about how different Cassie's mother was from mine. My mom turned cartwheels! But Mrs. Copeland seemed sort of distant and formal. I wondered if she was always like this with Cassie. Or rather, Cassandra.

After a while Mrs. Copeland asked to work with Lauren alone. Cassie and Tara and I went into the living room, and Mrs. Copeland closed the conservatory door. From time to time we could hear Lauren making loud, low noises.

"She sounds like a sick cow!" Tara laughed. Then,

growing serious, she added, "Just listening to your mother's speaking voice gives me chills. I'd love to hear her sing."

Cassie looked sad. "She never sings anymore. She used to, when I was little, but I can barely remember." Then, brightening a bit, she added, "Anyway, I knew she'd be able to help us with our voices. Especially Lauren."

Tara and I followed Cassie upstairs to her room then. She had a really cool four-poster bed and lots of bookcases. All her furniture was made of dark wood and looked old. She seemed proudest of her walk-in closet, where all her fabulous clothes hung in neat rows.

Cassie put on a Reba McEntire CD, and she and I sang along with a couple of her sad country love songs while Tara circled the room, checking out every picture, every book.

"This looks more like a library than a bedroom," Tara said at last. "And where do you keep your dirty clothes? They're not all over the floor, the way mine are."

Cassie wrinkled her nose at the idea. "I couldn't live if I weren't well organized," she said, walking over to her CDs, which were alphabetized by artist along the shelf. "Wait until you hear this," she told me. "It's classic Tammy Wynette."

About half an hour later Lauren burst into Cassie's room. "I got it!" she announced. "No kidding. I could feel my breath coming from way down deep, and my voice sounded completely different." She demonstrated: *"Go! Fight! Win!"*

"That's fantastic!" cried Tara, and we all hugged her.

"We're supposed to go back down to the conservatory now," Lauren told us. "Mrs. Copeland is going to serve tea."

We returned to the sunny, plant-filled room, where now classical music was playing. We sat down on the wicker couches again and waited.

"Your mother is the greatest teacher!" Lauren exclaimed.

"I'd *love* to study singing here," Tara said, half to herself.

Cassie became serious. "You know," she began, "I never . . . I mean, I don't invite anyone over much."

"Why not?" asked Tara. "You've got the perfect house. If I lived here, I'd have parties every single weekend!"

"Not if you lived here with my parents, you wouldn't," Cassie said. "They pretty much keep to themselves."

My curiosity took over. "Cassie, you know how you told me your mother *made* you come to cheerleading clinic?"

Cassie nodded solemnly.

"But your mother doesn't seem like a pom-pon mom."

"A *what?*" said Cassie.

"You know, one of those moms who pushes her little girl into cheering." I laughed. "Like *my* mom."

Everybody laughed at that one.

"Oh, right, Patti," teased Tara. "Your mom really had to tie you up and *drag* you to clinic."

"You know what I mean." I turned to Cassie. "Did your mother really talk you into trying out for cheerleading?"

Cassie nodded again. "I couldn't believe it either when she first brought it up, but then she explained that she thinks cheering might help me because I have some leadership ability, but—" Her face got a bit red as she admitted this. "I need to work on getting along with people."

"Keep working on it!" Tara joked as both Mr. and Mrs. Copeland appeared, carrying trays.

Mrs. Copeland set down her tray in front of us. "Just put yours here, Gregory," she told her husband. "Thank you, dear."

*"Bon appétit!"* said Mr. Copeland as he left.

One tray held a fancy silver teapot, four delicate blue china cups and saucers with gold rims, and four large cloth napkins. The other held silverware, a plate with tiny sandwiches, and another plate with equally small pastries.

"Whoa!" exclaimed Tara. "This looks just like the kind of tea they serve on those British programs on public television!"

Smiling, Mrs. Copeland poured the tea. She warned us not to take too much milk because it could cause congestion and affect our voices. She served us sandwiches with little silver tongs.

This was the fanciest party I'd ever been to! I watched Cassie to see what she did. So did Tara and Lauren. When Cassie took a napkin from the tray, we all reached for one. When she opened it and spread it out on her lap, we did that too. Somehow by following her example, we managed to look polite.

"The sandwiches look great, Mrs. Copeland," said Tara.

"Do try the watercress," said Mrs. Copeland, pointing to a section of the tray, "and these are tomato sandwiches, and these are cucumber."

Imagine eating those salady things on separate little squares and triangles of bread! At our house we'd just throw them all together—probably on top of a burger!

While we ate and drank our tea, Mrs. Copeland asked us more questions. They weren't the kinds of questions my mom asked, like what color socks the high school cheerleaders were wearing. She asked important things, like what we thought about the six women who had been elected to the Senate in the last election. (We thought it was good.) And what we thought about violence in our culture. (We thought it was bad.) She even asked if we had any solutions for this problem. (We said we'd think about it.)

I was sorry when six o'clock came and the tea ended.

We all thanked Mrs. Copeland. Lauren thanked her over and over and promised to practice breathing from her diaphragm.

"Best of luck at the tryouts," said Mrs. Copeland as she walked us to the door. "If I can be of help again, let me know."

Instead of waiting for us in the van, Mom had come up to the door. I knew she was dying to meet the Copelands and take a peek inside their house!

When Cassie introduced her parents, Mom said, "I sure am happy to meet you all!"

Boy, did she ever sound loud after the quiet Copelands!

"I'll see you Monday morning," Cassie called after us. "Eight thirty sharp!"

On the way home we told Mom all the details.

We dropped Tara off first in front of the Lakeview apartments. As she got out of the van she said, "You know, I don't think Mrs. Copeland has agoraphobia."

"You don't?" said Lauren.

"No," said Tara. "If I lived in that big, beautiful house, I'd never want to go out either."

# CHAPTER
# 13

"**D**ad dropped me off on his way to the station," Cassie announced as she stood on our front porch at a quarter to eight on Monday morning, holding a large roll of poster paper. "It's not too early, is it?"

"Oh, no," I told her. What else could I say? "Come on in."

"Hi, Cassie!" Mom called out as we walked into the kitchen. "Would you like some juice, honey? How about some toast?"

"No, thank you," Cassie said. "But Mrs. Richardson, I was wondering if you'd look over the schedule I've made. From my books on cheering, I think it's got everything we need to practice, but I'd like your opinion."

Cassie slipped off a rubber band and unrolled her poster.

### TRAINING CAMP SCHEDULE
*Monday, August 17–Friday, August 2–8*
8:30 a.m.     Arrive promptly at Richardsons'
              Warm-up—stretching and cheerobics

| 8:45 a.m. | Practice arm movements |
| 9:00 a.m. | Practice jumps |
| 9:45 a.m. | Practice partner stunts |
| 10:45 a.m. | Smile workshop |
| 11:00 a.m. | Mrs. Richardson's coaching session |
| 12:30 p.m. | Lunch |
| 1:00 p.m. | Advanced smile workshop |
| 1:15 p.m. | Spirit run |
| 2:00 p.m. | Cheers and chants |
| 2:45 p.m. | Voice projection practice |
| 3:15 p.m. | Positive-thinking session |
| 3:30 p.m. | Mock tryout—Mrs. Richardson, judge |
| 4:30 p.m. | Critique session |
| 5:30 p.m. | Work on weaknesses pointed out in critique |
| 7:00 p.m. | Dismissal |

Mom's eyes opened wide as she read. "Cassie, honey," she said when she'd finished, "with your schedule and my coaching, I think we're going to see some *real* progress."

"But there aren't any breaks!" Tara objected when she walked into the cartwheel room around nine and saw Cassie's schedule taped to the mirror. She had on black bike shorts and a turquoise halter top with six inches of bare midriff showing.

"The smile workshops and the positive-thinking session are really breaks," said Cassie. "And why are you so late?"

Tara groaned. "There's no way I'm going to make

91

it here at eight thirty every morning. Can't we *please* start later?"

"No," insisted Cassie. "Stretch out, Tara."

Tara glanced over at Lauren, who seemed quite comfortable with her legs extended sideways in Russian splits, and then at me, lying on my back with one leg flat on the floor, holding the other leg up over my head. As Cassie slid slowly into the splits Tara just stood there, looking miserable.

Lauren hopped up. She and Tara went off to a far corner and began talking and stretching quietly together. Once I thought I heard Lauren whisper, "Don't let her get to you." The two of them stayed off by themselves until Missy ran into the room.

"Why aren't you all practicing jumps?" she asked. "Is it time for me to be the very strict cheerleading coach now?"

"It's the perfect time, Missy," I told her.

Was it ever! Missy didn't even try to hide the fact that Tara was her favorite. She complimented her like crazy, and Tara's bad mood vanished. When the time for the smile workshop rolled around, we actually felt like smiling.

"Let's start by smiling at ourselves in the mirror," Cassie directed. "Then we'll smile while we cheer."

We all sat down close to the mirror and started grinning at ourselves. It wasn't that easy.

Tara giggled first. "It's so weird! When I stare at my smile, my teeth start looking like skinny marshmallows!"

"I felt like a wild beast baring its teeth," said Lauren.

"You *would* think about animals!" exclaimed Cassie,

and then she grew thoughtful. "Maybe we have to think of things that make us happy, and then our smiles will be real. Let's try again."

"I'm thinking of a Bingo's pizza," Tara murmured through the clenched teeth of her smile. "And of sharing it with T.D."

"I'm thinking of a big batch of Gram's chocolate chip cookies," said Lauren, "and of sharing them with *nobody*." She giggled. "At our house, that could never happen."

"I'm thinking of the number-four special from Taco Palace," I said, suddenly superhungry for Mexican food. "A big cheesy bean burrito with yellow rice and refried beans."

"Raspberry sorbet," said Cassie, "with a sprig of mint."

Suddenly we were smiling for real as we hopped up and ran from the cartwheel room straight for the refrigerator.

"Ready when you are," Mom said that afternoon as she stuck the score sheets Cassie had made into her clipboard.

The four of us stood in a corner of the cartwheel room. At a signal from Cassie we began our spirit run.

Mom took notes like crazy.

Then we each did the required individual cheer. Lauren looked great—and she sounded pretty good. Cassie had improved, and I thought I had too. Then came Tara's turn. Her hand motions looked sharper, and she cheered in a loud, clear voice:

*Touchdown! Touchdown! That's our goal!*
*Get that ball and take control!*
*Go, Lions! Go, go, go!*

But when Tara jumped, Mom looked worried. And that made me worry. What if Tara just couldn't get her jump working?

After Mom watched our partner stunts and our original group cheer, she filled out the score sheet. "I couldn't very well rate you in appearance today," Mom said, handing us the sheet.

0 = POOR; 1 = FAIR; 2 = AVERAGE; 3 = GOOD; 4 = SUPERIOR

|  | #1 L.A. | #2 C.C. | #3 T.M. | #4 P.R. |
|---|---|---|---|---|
| APPEARANCE: | ? | ? | ? | ? |
| VOICE: | 2 | 3 | 4 | 3 |
| JUMPS: | 4 | 3 | 1 | 4 |
| CHEER MOTIONS: | 4 | 3 | 2 | 2 |
| GYMNASTICS: | 4 | 2 | 1 | 4 |

GROUP SPIRIT RUN:  3
GROUP CHEER:  1

Mom hadn't given any zeros. It just wasn't in her to do that. But she'd scored us as tough as the judges at school.

"A *one* in the group cheer!" exclaimed Tara.

"It's a fine cheer," said Mom, "but it needs a lot of work on smoothness and timing. She looked at our disappointed faces. "So," she said, cheerful as ever, "let's get to work!"

Just after six that night, my dad arrived home and came into the cartwheel room. After smooching with Mom he said, "Say, do you girls know the joke about the man who got lost in New York City?"

"Dad!" I cried. "Don't you dare tell that joke!"

"Come on!" everybody else begged. "Tell us, Mr. Richardson!"

And so he did, ending with "Practice, practice, practice!"

Then everybody groaned.

My dad just grinned. "Well, how's your practice going?"

"Pretty well, Mr. Richardson," Cassie answered, "but we've got a long way to go." She frowned. "I wish there were more hours in the day so we could practice more."

"You know, you can practice more." He tapped his head with his finger. "Up here."

"How?" Cassie asked, getting all excited. "Tell us how!"

"Dad," I said, "is this another one of your awful jokes?"

"Nope," he said. "It's the absolute truth. When I was playing football for U.T., one of our guards, Brian Gilpin, got hurt and ended up in the hospital in a body cast. From the neck down, he couldn't move for six weeks. Now old Brian knew he had to do something to keep his mind occupied, so he decided to teach himself touch typing."

"I thought he couldn't move his arms," Lauren said.

"He couldn't," said Dad. "He asked his nurse to get him a typing book, and she rigged up a reading stand for him."

"How'd old Brian turn the pages?" asked Tara.

"By holding a tongue depressor stick between his teeth," Dad explained. "So every day old Brian read one typing lesson and practiced—in his head. When they removed his body cast, he got himself a typewriter, and sure enough, old Brian could type."

"Is this true?" Cassie asked.

"Well, I don't know that Brian broke any speed records," said Dad, "but it's true. When you think-practice an activity, your brain makes the same connections that it would make if you were actually practicing."

Cassie was already writing down Brian Gilpin's story.

Cassie had decided that our cheerleading camp would end at seven each evening. At that hour it was still light enough for Lauren and Tara to bike home, and it just happened to be the perfect time for her father to pick her up on his way home from the station.

"Hey, Dad," I said as everybody started gathering up their things that night, "it's too bad old Brian didn't teach himself to play the piano while he was in that body cast."

"Why's that?" asked my dad.

" 'Cause with all that practice, practice, practice," I told him, "I bet he could have gotten to Carnegie Hall!"

# CHAPTER
## 14

"Why don't we have lunch *alfresco* today?" Cassie suggested on Wednesday as she looked out the window. The day was sunny but not too hot. On Monday and Tuesday we'd done nothing but practice, and we were all sick of being inside.

"Al who?" said Tara.

*"Alfresco,"* said Cassie. "It's Italian, and it means outside in the fresh air."

"In plain English, Cassie," I said, "I think you're suggesting a picnic."

And so at lunchtime we spread a quilt out on the grass in the backyard and sat down on it to eat our sandwiches. We hadn't been sitting there more than a minute when Missy zoomed out the back door, carrying her little red plastic lunch box.

"Can I come on the picnic too?" she asked.

"Sure," said Tara, patting the spot next to her.

Missy sat down and looked over at Cassie's sandwich. "What is *that?*" she asked.

"Alfalfa sprouts and cream cheese on date nut bread," Cassie told her.

"It looks yucky," Missy said.

"It isn't," said Cassie. "Would you like to try a bite?"

"No way. I like ham sandwiches." Missy took a big bite of her own ham sandwich.

"I'm a vegetarian," Cassie said, "so I don't eat meat."

"Hey, me neither!" said Lauren. "I *hate* the idea of killing animals for food."

"What animals?" asked Missy.

"Like cows for hamburgers," Lauren said, "and pigs for ham."

Missy stopped chewing.

"Missy?" I said. "Are you okay?"

Miss shook her head. Her eyes filled with tears.

"Do you want to spit out that bite you took?" I asked. Missy nodded yes.

"Go ahead," I told her. "It's okay."

But she couldn't seem to do it until I put my hand up in front of her mouth to catch her chewed-up bite. The minute it was out of her mouth, she started crying loudly. "I'm sorry, piggy!"

"I'm the one who's sorry, Missy," said Lauren. I could tell she really felt bad. "I thought you knew where ham came from."

"Here." Cassie held out one of her little date-nut triangles to Missy. "I bet you'll like this."

Sniffling, Missy took it and started nibbling around the nuts. "I'm going to be a vegetable-tarian too," she said.

After we finished eating, Missy went off to find Mom

and explain her new eating habits, and the four of us lay back on the quilt and just stared into space for a while. The sky was blue, and a gentle breeze was blowing. I felt happy. Cassie and Tara hadn't had a single argument all morning. At that moment it didn't seem too much to hope that our team problems were behind us now, and we could just practice, practice, practice.

But the next morning, Tara twirled into the cartwheel room around eleven. She wore a black halter top with hot pink polka dots and black leggings with hot pink stripes. From one earlobe dangled a pink bowling pin and from the other, a little black bowling ball. "Could this be perfect for tryouts?" she asked.

"No!" Lauren and I cried together.

"Ha!" said Tara. "Gotcha! Come on, guys, you didn't really think I'd wear something like this to tryouts, did you?"

"Yes!" we both exclaimed.

During Tara's fashion show, Cassie didn't say a word. She just stood with her arms crossed on her chest. "Tara," she said at last, "you're *over two hours late!*"

"Oh, no!" Tara was clearly acting upset. "Did I miss ten minutes of smiling at myself in the mirror?"

"As a matter of fact," shouted Cassie, jabbing her finger in the direction of her schedule, "you missed stretching, arm movements, jumps, partner stunts, *and* smile workshop!"

Tara looked grim. "We're not trying out for the Miss America Pageant, Cassie. I think we could cut smiling practice."

Cassie looked furious. "It's not just smiling, it's spirit. And it's important! Your toe-touch jump is an embarrassment! You should be practicing the hardest of anybody!"

"Get a grip, Cassie," advised Tara. "This is cheerleading, not brain surgery. Maybe you should make a few changes in that sacred schedule of yours so it would work for all of us."

"And maybe you should think about Lauren! She can't practice partner stunts if you're not here!" Cassie yelled.

Tara turned to Lauren. "Sorry, partner," she said.

Lauren just shrugged. "We can do our stunts after lunch."

But the bad feeling between Cassie and Tara took all the fun out of practice that day. Everything we did seemed like plain hard work. On Friday, Tara arrived after ten. Cassie was boiling. None of us was having a good time.

Friday night Cassie phoned me. "Listen, Patti," she said, "I've really had it with Tara—her lateness, her bad attitude, her terrible jumps."

"I know," I said, "but—"

"But nothing," Cassie interrupted. "Tryouts are a week from tomorrow! What about our group cheer? Our unison toe-touch jump is a mess! I don't want my score brought down because Tara just can't bother to get it together."

Suddenly Cassie reminded me of Darcy Lewis!

"Kelsey McGee was on the Heights squad last year," Cassie went on. "She and I weren't exactly friends or anything, but I bet if I called her, she'd come over and practice with us."

"But Cassie, Tara's part of our team."

"Then she should act like it," said Cassie. "If Tara's late tomorrow, I'm calling Kelsey."

I didn't know what else to say. We hung up then, and I lay on my bed for a while, thinking.

Tara had been my first friend in Paxton. She'd kept Darcy from making fun of me. And when I'd been the only one whooping in the gym, she'd whooped along with me. I owed her a lot. And I really liked Tara. She made everything seem like so much fun.

I liked Cassie too, even if she was bossy when it came to organizing things. And I understood that it wasn't easy to be working hard on a team when one team member was goofing off.

I wondered if maybe Tara acted as if she didn't care because she didn't want to try her hardest and *still* not be able to do a good toe-touch jump. I didn't know. But I kept thinking. I just had to figure out a way to save our team. Our *whole* team.

I phoned Tara just after seven on Saturday morning and woke her up. I asked her please to be at my house by eight thirty.

"It's important, Tara," I said.

"All right," she grumbled. "I'll be there."

And she was.

"Surprise, surprise," Cassie said as she looked up from the floor of the cartwheel room, where she and

Lauren had been stretching since eight. "Look who's here."

"Hi, Tara!" called Missy as she and Mom appeared in the doorway.

"Listen, girls," Mom said, "Missy and I are going out for a while. Daddy's upstairs if you need anything."

"Okay," I said. "Where are you going?"

"Oh, just somewhere," said Missy, looking up at Mom as if the two of them were sharing the world's biggest secret.

After they left, I said, "Come sit over here for a minute, guys. We've got something to take care of."

I'd thought Cassie might object to doing something that wasn't on the schedule, but she didn't.

Tara sat on a pillow to my left. Lauren sat next to Tara, and Cassie sat on my right. I held up my old home run softball. On it I'd drawn a face and hair. "This is Dr. Donna," I said.

"Hi ya, Doc," said Tara.

"Oh, puh-lease!" Cassie muttered.

Lauren giggled. "What kind of doctor is Donna?" she asked.

"A shrink," Tara suggested.

"Right," I said. "Dr. Donna is our team psychologist, and she's going to help us get back our team spirit."

I tried to ignore Cassie rolling her eyes.

"We pass Dr. Donna around," I continued. "When you get Dr. Donna, if you have anything to say, say it. Only the person holding Dr. Donna can talk—no interrupting."

I handed Dr. Donna to Tara. Without a word, she

gave the ball to Lauren. Lauren gave it to Cassie. And the silence ended.

"I have plenty to say," she announced, and started talking a mile a minute about Tara letting us down and Tara not being part of the team. Tara's face turned red, but she didn't interrupt.

Finally Cassie handed Dr. Donna back to me. I took a deep breath. "Cassie," I said, "it was your idea for us to practice together, and it was a great idea. But I don't like the way you try to make us do everything just because you want us to. We have to do things because we feel like a team."

I gave Dr. Donna to Tara then, and she rolled the ball over and over in her hands. At last she said, "Getting up early is really hard for me."

"Oh, give me a break!" Cassie said.

Lauren surprised us all by shouting, "Don't interrupt!"

"The reason it's hard," Tara went on, "is because I stay up late, and the reason I stay up late is because my mom works until ten." Tara looked around at us. "You've heard the ads on the radio for Sabrina's Salon, right? 'The nighttime beauty stop for today's working woman'? My mom cuts hair at Sabrina's, and when she gets off work, she picks up dinner and brings it home. Lots of times we don't eat until eleven, and then we talk and watch TV."

Cassie looked down at her lap now.

"Anyway, my mom sleeps late. During the school year I hardly ever get to see her, so in the summer I like to wait up." Tara handed Dr. Donna to Lauren.

Lauren took Dr. Donna. Then she leaned over and

gave Tara a big hug. While the two of them were hugging, Cassie reached over and grabbed the ball from Lauren.

"Listen," she said as a single tear rolled down her cheek, "I'm really sorry, Tara. I didn't know. We can change the schedule. I was just trying to make us . . ."

Lauren grabbed the ball back. "That's just it, Cassie. You're always trying to *make us* do things."

Cassie nodded.

"But," Tara said, holding up her hands so that Lauren could toss her the ball, "if Cassie hadn't made a schedule, I probably would have slept half the day away. And I didn't want to do that. I really need to make the squad."

"Need to?" I asked, forgetting all about Dr. Donna.

Tara sighed. "Eva, the manicurist at Sabrina's, is a good friend of ours, and she gave Mom this article about a college that has a great theater program—you know how I want to be an actor. Anyway, this college gives cheerleading scholarships. Mom showed me the article, and I know I make up good cheers, and I love to dance, and have a loud voice, so I figured—hey! All I'd have to do is learn a few cheers, and I could get one." She smiled. "But now that I've had a little taste of cheerleading, I think it'd be a lot easier to study day and night and get a math scholarship!"

We all laughed.

Then Tara's smile faded. "But I don't want to cause any more problems," she said. "I mean, so what if I get here every morning at eight thirty? My toe-touch jump is still lousy. I can't do the splits. Let's face it, I'm just not in the same league with the rest of you guys, and I don't want to hold you back."

Tara stood up suddenly and said, "So count me out."

"What are you doing?" I asked.

"Leaving." Tara turned and walked out of the room.

"Wait! Tara!" I jumped to my feet and ran after her. So did Lauren. But Tara ran faster. She burst out our front door and ran down the walk as fast as she could go.

# CHAPTER
# 15

"Tara!" I called. But Tara just kept running. I turned to Lauren, who stood on the porch beside me. "I'm going after her!"

"Don't." Lauren put a hand on my arm. "I know Tara, and when she gets like this, she needs time to cool down."

We just stood there on the porch. The sun was high in the sky—it was only around ten—but already it felt as if it had been a long day. Slowly we walked back to the cartwheel room. Cassie was sitting on a pillow, looking very lonely.

We sat down too. For a while no one spoke.

At last Cassie said, "It's true, you know."

"What's true?" I asked.

"What Tara said. That she isn't as good as the rest of us. She really could have brought down our scores at tryouts."

"Cassie, that doesn't matter," Lauren said softly.

"Doesn't matter?" Cassie looked surprised. "Of

course it matters! Listen, I'll call Kelsey McGee and I'm sure she'll—"

"No!" I shouted in a voice that any judge would rate a four. "You sound just as horrible as Darcy Lewis!" All the anger I'd felt at Darcy boiled up in me now and spilled out at Cassie.

"What's she got to do with this?" Cassie looked confused.

Near tears, I told Cassie and Lauren what Darcy had said that last day of clinic—how she'd been willing to kick Sarah out of her group just because she'd seen someone better.

"I still don't get it," Cassie said when I was finished.

"If we let Tara go," I tried to explain, "and we call up Kelsey to replace her, then we're just like Darcy!"

"No, we're not," Cassie insisted. "We didn't kick Tara out. She quit."

"But she quit so she wouldn't hurt us," Lauren said.

"We're a team, remember?" I folded my arms across my chest. "And Tara's my friend. If deserting your friends is what it takes to make the squad, then I don't want to be a Paxton cheerleader."

"I don't either," Lauren agreed.

Cassie looked from me to Lauren and back again. Then she sighed. "As I see it," she said, "we have two choices. Either we all practice alone and let Mrs. Holland assign us to a group at tryouts or we find a way to get Tara back—a way that works."

"Besides starting later," Lauren said, "the only thing that will work is if Tara really believes in herself."

Cassie found the last score sheet that Mom had filled

out. "Her cheer motions have improved," she told us. "So has her gymnastics score. But her toe-touch jump's still only a two."

"Hey, Lauren," I said suddenly. "Maybe Salleen could give her some private coaching."

Lauren shook her head. "Salleen's staying with her cousins in Chicago. She won't be back until Friday."

We sat there for a while, thinking of ways to help Tara—if we could get her to come back. It was a big *if*.

"Oh, hello, Mrs. Richardson," Cassie said.

"Howdy, girls," someone said.

I looked up and gasped. "Aunt Peggy!" I cried.

Mom appeared beside her sister and said, "Surprise!"

I ran over and hugged my aunt while Missy jumped around us chanting, "I knew she was coming! I knew she was coming!"

"Peggy's here for a whole week," Mom said, beaming. "I can't wait to show her Paxton and Chicago."

"This is my aunt, Mrs. Yoxall," I told Cassie and Lauren.

"Wow, Mrs. Yoxall," said Lauren, "you and Mrs. Richardson are really identical."

Aunt Peggy smiled. "You girls call me Aunt Peggy."

"Where's Tara?" asked Missy.

When none of us answered, Mom said, "What's wrong?"

And so I explained. "I know Tara doesn't want to quit," I said at last. "If there was only some way she could believe her toe-touch was getting better, I think she'd come back."

Mom nodded. "Tara's been working hard, but nothing's happened for a while. She's due for a big break-through."

"You girls ask Tara to come back," Aunt Peggy said, winking at Mom, "and next week Sunny and I'll take care of her jump."

"Whooo-eeee!" Mom whooped. "Will we ever!"

"But what about your sightseeing trips?" asked Cassie.

"Oh, I can see Chicago on my next visit," said Aunt Peggy.

"Hey, wait," I said. "What if you coach Tara in the mornings and then we'll work with her in the afternoons?"

"That's perfect, Patti, honey!" exclaimed Mom. "Now go get Tara and smooth things over. Go on, girls! Get a move on!"

Before we had time to think, Lauren and Cassie and I were walking to Tara's apartment. I'd thought maybe Cassie would say she shouldn't come, but she didn't. She seemed all excited about the challenge of getting Tara's toe-touch jump in shape and about having *two* private coaches.

When we reached the Lakeview apartments—four white, three-story brick buildings that formed a square—Cassie and I followed Lauren into the center courtyard, where there was a big, beautiful pool.

"You think Tara's had enough time to cool off?" I asked Lauren as we reached apartment 3B.

Lauren shrugged. "Hope so," she said, and knocked.

"Who is it?" Tara called.

"Us!" Lauren called back. "Your friends."

I heard footsteps and the door swung open. Tara stood behind it, her eyes puffy from crying.

"You're late!" she joked, letting us in.

Tara's apartment was as colorful as her outfits. We sat on a pair of grass green couches dotted with bright throw pillows. Wild jungle-pattern cloths covered the tables, and on the walls were framed prints of brilliant flowers.

"Listen," Cassie began, "we have a week till tryouts—"

"What Cassie means, Tara," I quickly interrupted, "is that we need you back to be a team."

"No, you don't," said Tara.

"We do," Lauren insisted.

"But my toe-touch—" began Tara.

Now Cassie interrupted. "Your jump is going to be fine," she said. "You're going to have two private coaches, and Mrs. Richardson said you'd been working really hard on your jump and she expected a big improvement any minute."

Tara looked from Cassie to Lauren and said, "Huh?"

And so Lauren explained about Aunt Peggy and her idea. "Please come back, Tara," Lauren said at last. "Please."

Tara got teary again. "I would, really, but I can't."

"Why not?" asked Cassie.

"On Monday my mom's going to this big hairstylists' convention." Tara sniffed. "In Atlanta. Eva, who works with my mom, was going to stay with me, but now she's going too, so I'm going to my dad's. It's all arranged."

"Stay with me!" Lauren offered.

"No," said Cassie.

We all looked at her, surprised.

"I only meant," Cassie said, "that you should stay at Patti's. That way you'd be living with your coaches."

I laughed. "I haven't agreed with much that Cassie's said lately, but I think she's right." I looked at Tara. "We'd love to have you stay with us. Between Mom and Aunt Peggy you may not know what hit you, but if you want to work on your jump, my house is the perfect place to be."

Tara grinned. "Okay," she said. "Count me in."

Tara and I phoned our moms and got okays for her to stay over. "Mom says to tell you to keep stretching," I said as I hung up. "She wants you to be as limber as possible on Monday morning when she gets ahold of you."

"Ouch," said Tara. "Hey, I've got an idea. Let's go swimming!"

Several minutes later the four of us made our way down to the Lakeview pool. I fit into one of Tara's colorful two-piece suits just fine, and Lauren fit into a red tank suit. But Cassie was so small that Tara had to dig around in her drawers until she came up with a suit she said she'd worn in fourth grade!

We had the best time that afternoon. There weren't many people in the pool, so we could play Marco Polo and Jump/Dive without anyone complaining that we were too loud. After the games we had races, and I beat everybody in backstroke.

"You know, Tara," Cassie said as we stood in the shallow end just talking, "you can do great stretches in the water."

"Don't start . . ." growled Tara.

"Sorry." Cassie sighed. "I realize my drive to direct everything can be a little much at times."

"Cassie!" I exclaimed. "In your own way, I think you just admitted that you're too bossy!"

# CHAPTER
# 16

**H**owdy, Tara," Aunt Peggy said on Monday morning after Tara's mom dropped her at our house with what looked like enough luggage for a round-the-world trip.

After I helped Tara settle into my room, we went back down to the cartwheel room. There Mom and Aunt Peggy—and Coach Missy, of course—asked Tara to smile, bend, stretch, kick, jump, do hand motions, do splits, and jump some more.

"Why do I feel like a horse that's for sale?" Tara asked as Aunt Peggy circled her one last time, checking every angle.

Mom turned to me. "Patti, would you run into the kitchen and get us a chair, please?"

Then Mom showed Tara how to hold on to the back of the chair and practice springing. "When you spring, take off from the balls of your feet," Mom said. "jump up, and when you're in the air, then spread your legs out as wide as you can. Now, try it."

Tara tried. Mom and Aunt Peggy watched closely. "Okay, that's fine," Aunt Peggy said. "Just keep those toes pointed."

"I'll never do this." Tara shook her head.

"No negativity!" Mom insisted. "I can tell you've got it in you to do a jump that'll knock those judges' socks off!"

Tara grinned. "You really think so, Mrs. Richardson?"

Mom put her hands on her hips. "When it comes to cheerleading, Tara, honey, I *know* what I'm talking about."

It may have been my imagination, but after that it really did seem as if Tara's jump got a little better.

When Cassie and Lauren arrived, Mom and Aunt Peggy took Tara into the living room for a "private session." Not until they went into town for lunch did Tara come back to practice with us. Actually it was less like practice and more like coaching Tara—who already looked sort of worn out.

"Jump again," said Cassie, watching like a hawk. "Aha!" she cried. "You're doing one-jump prep."

"You're right!" Lauren exclaimed. "Salleen showed me how to do a two-jump prep." She turned to Tara. "You won't believe how much more height two little jumps can give you."

"Melody did a two-jump prep," I said. "But I could never get the hang of it."

"You mean it's hard to switch from one to two?" asked Tara.

"It was for me because I'd been doing it my old way

for so long," I told her. "But you just learned to jump a couple of weeks ago, so it won't be so hard for you."

But I was wrong. At first when Tara tried it, her jump fell apart. By the time Mom and Aunt Peggy returned home around six, she was just starting to get better.

"By George, I think I've got it," Tara said in her best English accent. "The prep, that is."

"Go ahead, Tara, honey," said Mom. "Show us your stuff."

Tara stood in the center of the cartwheel room. She got her concentration, did the new prep, and jumped.

Mom and Aunt Peggy whooped and hollered when she landed.

Tara still had a ways to go, but this jump was a definite improvement.

Cassie took out her notebook and made some notes.

"Just be sure to write down how close my head was to the ceiling," Tara told her, flopping down on a pillow.

Cassie looked up. "I'm not sure our unison jump is ever going to work," she said. "I was thinking that maybe we should try a ripple, with jumps staggered one right after the other."

"Tomorrow," moaned Tara.

"Come on!" Cassie pulled Tara up. "Lowest jump goes first. That's you, Tara."

Did Cassie have to be so blunt? I thought as we lined up.

"Tara goes on the count of one," Cassie said. "I'll go on two, Patti on three, and Lauren on four. Okay, ready, *and!*"

"One!" she called, and Tara jumped. "Two!" Cassie

jumped. "Three!" I jumped. "Four!" Lauren did our finale.

"Hey!" We all looked at each other. It wasn't the greatest ripple jump in the history of cheerleading, but it wasn't bad. It made me feel hopeful that we could get it in shape for tryouts.

Cassie smiled. "That's called the ripple flying splits," she told us. "If we can do it as part of the original cheer at tryouts, we'll definitely impress the judges!"

That night after dinner Tara and I went up to my room.

"Want to have a MASH session?" she asked.

"Nope," I said, slipping a video into my VCR.

"Okay," said Tara, "I can definitely get into watching a movie. What is it?"

"It's something Mom ordered from one of her catalogs just for you," I told her as I pressed *play*.

"Aaaaahhh! A horror film!" Tara screamed as the title *Improving Your Toe-Touch Jump* appeared on the screen.

"Let's stretch while we watch," I suggested.

"You're getting just as bossy as Cassie," Tara told me as she sat down on the floor beside me.

"Don't complain," I said. "Or I'll put the tape on slow motion!"

For the next three days all our lives were totally focused on cheering tryouts. Mom and Aunt Peggy didn't even go sightseeing in the afternoons.

"To tell the truth," Aunt Peggy said, "I'd rather be right here with my girls!"

I believed her.

Lauren and Cassie went home at seven each evening, but for Tara and me cheerleading camp continued. For dinner Mom cooked high-carbohydrate recipes that Cassie had copied from a book called *Eat for Energy*. We never sat down without putting our legs out in a wide *V* and stretching. Before we went to bed, we closed our eyes and Dad talked us through mental toe-touch jumps, courtesy of Brian Gilpin. Missy even claimed that she heard Tara yelling *Go, Lions! Go! Go! Go!* in her sleep.

Late on Thursday afternoon, Tara's mom phoned to say she was back from Atlanta. We all went to my room while Tara packed up her things.

"I'm wiped out," Tara said. "I feel like one of those sleepwalking characters from some old episode of 'The Twilight Zone.'"

"We do need a break," admitted Cassie.

"If you're saying that, Cassie," I said, "it must be true!"

"Patti, may I use your phone?" asked Lauren. When she came back from making her call, she was smiling. "Everyone's invited to my house for breakfast tomorrow morning. Ten o'clock sharp."

We picked up Cassie the next morning a little before ten, and Mom dropped us off downtown at Lauren's house, a big, square red brick building. Lauren's parents had their offices on the first floor of the house, so we ran up a set of steps to her front door on the second floor. As we did we almost got bowled over by a little boy and girl running down the steps.

"You'll meet Amy and Gary next time," Lauren told us as she stood at the door. "They were late for their camp bus."

We followed her down a hallway to a big, sunny kitchen that smelled of apples and cinnamon. "Gram, I'd like you to meet Patti Richardson and Cassie Copeland," Lauren said to a tall woman with snow white hair. "This is my grandmother, Mrs. Webster."

"How do you do?" I said, and shook her hand.

"I'm so happy to meet you," said Mrs. Webster.

Tara arrived about ten minutes later. "Wait till you hear my news!" she exclaimed. "Boy, does it ever smell great in here!"

Mrs. Webster smiled. "I hope you'll think my pancakes taste as good as they smell," she said as we sat down at the table.

"What's your news, Tara?" Lauren asked as we started in on the big, puffy pancakes filled with steaming apple chunks.

"First of all, my mom won some award in Atlanta," Tara said.

"That's great!" we all told her.

Tara nodded. "Sabrina told my mom to take three days off with pay, but guess what else she asked for?"

"What?" asked Cassie.

"My mom asked if she could open the salon really early tomorrow morning, and Sabrina said yes, so my mom and Eva have invited the four of us in for a morning of beauty!"

"So we'll look great for tryouts!" exclaimed Lauren.

"Tara," said Cassie, "do you think they can tame my frizzies?"

"No problem," said Tara. "And manicures all around!"

I held out my fingernails to her.

"Eva can't work miracles, Patti," Tara teased, "but I'm sure she can make them look better. Plus Eva does makeup, so bring your blush and lipstick and whatever!"

"This is going to be great!" exclaimed Cassie.

Over and over we told Mrs. Webster how delicious her pancakes were. We ate them with plenty of butter and syrup, and had seconds and thirds. It was just what we needed.

After we washed the dishes, Lauren took us up to her room. It was on the fifth floor and was small and cozy. From one of her windows I could see the Paxton park.

"I stand at the window to do my daily yelling practice," Lauren told us. "All of Paxton has heard my deep, loud voice!"

Cassie studied the gymnastics trophies on Lauren's bookcase. "Very impressive," she said.

But Lauren showed us what she considered much more impressive. "This is Annie," she said stroking a calico cat curled up on her pillow. Then she opened her closet door a little more and we saw a large black-and-white cat staring down at us from the top shelf. "And that's Groucho," she said. "Harpo's around here somewhere. Hey—" She put a hand to her throat. "Did my voice sound funny?"

"Sort of," I told her.

Clearing her throat, she took a breath and in a deep but scratchy voice cheered: *"Go, Paxton, go! Fight, Paxton, fight!"*

"Lauren!" Cassie cried. "You're hoarse! You've been practicing too much!"

Lauren headed for the stairs, and we followed her all the way down to her dad's office. We sat in the waiting room with a bunch of moms and little kids, while Lauren slipped into an examining room so her father could look at her throat.

A few minutes later Lauren and her father, wearing a white coat, came out to the waiting room. Lauren looked miserable.

"Well, Lauren's throat is red and inflamed," Dr. Armstrong told us, "but I think it's from overdoing rather than from anything contagious."

"When I get a sore throat, Mother has me gargle with hot salt water," Cassie said. "Maybe that would help Lauren."

Dr. Armstrong looked amused at this advice from Dr. Cassie, but all he said was, "I think in this case voice rest is the best medicine."

Lauren popped one of the lozenges her father had given her into her mouth. She didn't way a word as we walked back to my house.

Mom and Aunt Peggy were waiting for us. So was Missy. We all went into the cartwheel room for one last mock tryout before the real thing.

"We're pretty full of pancakes," Tara warned our judges as they sat with score sheets in front of them.

Lauren motioned that she'd be doing silent cheers.

120

"Just do it," said Missy.

And we did.

Our final score sheet had a couple of surprises.

"You're kidding!" Tara looked from Mom to Aunt Peggy, her eyes shining. "My jump's a three? Really a *three?*"

"Three means good," said Aunt Peggy.

"That's how your jump looked to us, honey," added Mom.

Truthfully, I thought Tara's jump was still more in the two-and-a-half category, but I knew Mom and Aunt Peggy were trying to boost Tara's confidence. And the three sure did the trick. Tara boogied around the room, chanting, "Three! Three! Three!"

But that was before we noticed our group cheer score. It was a two. We looked at Mom and Aunt Peggy, puzzled.

"The timing's off," Mom said softly.

Cassie's face fell. "But tryouts are tomorrow!" she cried. "It's too late to change the ripple flying splits now!"

Mom hopped up and put an arm around Cassie. "This is like putting on a play, honey," she said. "Lots of times the dress rehearsal is just plain awful, and everybody thinks the play will never come together, and then, on opening night, everybody gives it their all and—bingo! It's a hit!"

"*A hit!*" Petey squawked from his cage.

But Cassie just shook her head. "This isn't a play," she said. "This is real. And I don't think it's ever coming together."

# CHAPTER
# 17

"Patti? Are you awake? It's tryout day."

My eyes popped open. Missy stood over my bed.

*Tryout day*—the day I'd been thinking of ever since last July in Texas when Mom first showed me the flyer about the clinic, ever since I heard those words *the Paxton cheerleaders*.

I headed for the bathroom, wondering: If I'd known everything that was going to happen—all the ups and downs and tears and making up—would I still have wanted to try out?

Like we used to say back home—you bet!

After a fast breakfast I packed up my lunch and my tryout clothes and Mom drove me over to Sabrina's Salon.

When I walked in, I saw that Lauren was already there and Eva was busy braiding her hair. Tara gave me a wave from where she sat under a dryer. Cassie hadn't arrived yet.

Tara's mom had a great, friendly smile. She was tall

and dark haired and wore an orange T-shirt and pink leggings. She showed me where to sit for my shampoo.

"Tara told me you like your hair in a French braid with just the lightest fringe of bangs," she said.

"Yes, ma'am," I replied.

Mrs. Miller began to wash my hair with a shampoo that smelled like roses. I leaned back and started to enjoy my morning of beauty.

Just as Mrs. Miller was finishing the most gorgeous French braid ever, the door to Sabrina's opened and Cassie charged in looking completely frantic. Her curly red hair wasn't up in its usual ponytail but sprang wildly from her head.

"Don't say it, Tara," she warned. "I know—I'm late!"

"Hello, Cassie," said Mrs. Miller. "I'm glad you're here."

"Thank you, Mrs. Miller," said Cassie. "And now . . . help!"

"My, my!" Mom exclaimed when she, Aunt Peggy, and Missy walked into Sabrina's Salon at nine thirty. "What a difference two hours can make!"

We had all changed into our tryout outfits: yellow T-shirts, white shorts, white socks, and white sneakers.

"Are we fabulous or what?" said Tara. Her extra-shiny dark hair was in a sleek ponytail tied with a bright blue ribbon.

Lauren gestured for Mom and Aunt Peggy to look at her hair, which Eva had styled in delicate cornrows.

"Look!" exclaimed Cassie, turning around. "No frizzies!"

Mom turned to me then. "Whooo-eeee! I thought I was the French braid queen," she said, "but I'll have to turn my title over to Mrs. Miller!"

I held out my hands so Mom could see my clear polish.

"Patti!" she exclaimed. "Your nails look . . . normal!"

We all had on just a little bit of blush, light lipstick, and Eva's special nonsmear mascara—the kind that doesn't get all messy if you accidentally rub your eyes.

We hopped into the van and headed for the junior high. When we pulled up to the curb, the four of us jumped out. As we started for the gym Mom, Aunt Peggy, and Missy yelled after us at the top of their lungs: "Don't smile!"

"Don't stick me!" wailed Tara.

"Then hold still," Cassie commanded. She'd already pinned a stiff card with a large number twenty-five to her own T-shirt and now she was trying to pin number twenty-six to Tara's shirt. I had twenty-seven and Lauren was wearing twenty-eight.

Looking around the gym, I saw Mrs. Holland and the other judges standing at their long table, fooling with a microphone. Everything looked the way it had that first day at clinic—only now no one was wearing cutoffs or sloppy T-shirts.

After we had our numbers on, we went over to the bleachers and sat in the same spot we had at mock try-outs. It didn't seem possible that two weeks had gone by since then. And it didn't seem possible that school would be starting in three days!

When Mrs. Holland got the microphone working, she

124

said, "Welcome to the seventh-grade cheerleading try-outs. Our judges today are Beth Ann Sorel, the squad coach; Dean Marzollo, head of our physical education department; and Rachel Garver, the PJHS drama teacher. I'd also like to introduce our squad trainer, Steve Liu, who will be standing by in case of injuries."

Steve Liu looked young enough to be in high school.

"He's cute," whispered Tara. "I wouldn't mind sprain-ing my ankle if he'd take care of it."

"Bite your tongue!" snapped Cassie.

"Salleen Cook, captain of the Paxton High School cheerleaders, and I will be running the tryouts today and tabulating the scores," Mrs. Holland said. "For those of you who attended the clinic, tryouts will feel familiar. First each girl will do a spirit run, the required cheer, and an optional cheer, which may be a standard cheer or one you've made up. Then we'll have partner cheers, and we'll finish with group cheers—we'll supply the words and your group will have ten minutes to supply the actions." She smiled. "We'll announce the results at five o'clock."

"Number one," called Salleen, "assume the on-deck position."

Standing in the far corner of the gymnasium was Darcy Lewis.

"Now performing," said Salleen, "number one."

Darcy sprinted to the center of the gym. We all clapped and yelled for her. I have to admit I held back my Texas best.

As Darcy was performing her excellent individual cheer, an awful thought struck me. What if I made the squad—and Darcy did too? Well, I thought with a smile, I could always bring out Dr. Donna!

Cassie sat on one side of me, whispering a positive-thinking lecture to herself. On my other side sat Lauren, who wasn't talking at all. Neither of them offered much comfort. Glancing at Tara, sitting beside Lauren, I saw that she was concentrating on stretching out her legs. I struggled to keep my polished nails away from my teeth as I watched girl after girl perform. It seemed like a long wait to number twenty-seven. But at least I was luckier than the girl I saw wearing number fifty-two!

Number seven. Number nineteen. Number twenty-two. Just before eleven o'clock Salleen called, "Number twenty-five to the on-deck position."

"Don't smile!" I whispered as Cassie jumped down from the bleachers and walked to the corner of the gym.

After number twenty-four finished, Salleen said, "Number twenty-six, assume the on-deck position."

I "don't smiled" Tara as she headed to the corner.

"Now performing," announced Salleen, "number twenty-five."

With that Cassie sprang forward as if she'd been fired from a cannon. As she flipped and cartwheeled her way across the gym floor, I began circling my right arm above my head and then let out a loud *yaaaa-hooo!* Cassie raised fantastic spirit, and all her smile workshops paid off. She looked like a pro.

While everyone yelled for Cassie, Salleen called my number.

"Don't smile, Patti," whispered Lauren.

"Hey, you talked!" I said as she gave my hand a

squeeze. I told her not to smile either. Then I was on my way.

From the corner of the gym I watched Tara. Her spirit run was full of excitement. She ended it, and then made a major goof. Instead of catching her breath and waiting for Salleen to give her the nod before starting the required cheer, Tara started right in. Suddenly she realized her mistake and stopped.

"Excuse me," Tara said in a calm voice, without making a silly face or looking flustered. "I started too soon. I'll wait until you give me the signal and begin again."

"Fine," said Salleen. And then she nodded.

Tara's required cheer looked good. But it was her optional cheer—obviously an original—that brought down the house.

> *Paxton Lions! That's our name!*
> *And tough is how we play the game!*

Tara had combined dance moves with cheering motions. She looked so tough and sassy that it made me want to laugh and cheer at the same time.

> *You'll hear us roar! Then see us score!*
> *Lions! Lions! We want more!*

On the word *more!* Tara did the best jump I'd ever seen her do! It definitely lived up to Mom and Aunt Peggy's three! Everyone erupted with cheering.

Tara's cheer had stirred up lots of energy. Now it was my turn to build on it and stir up lots more! When I heard Salleen call my number, I sprang out from the corner of the gym with a Texas-sized whoop and a holler. I just had to get every single girl in those bleachers whooping and hollering with me. And I did! As I turned cartwheels and flips I could feel everyone yelling with me for the Lions!

After the spirit run I stood there, panting. At a nod from Salleen, I went into the required cheer:

*Touchdown! Touchdown! That's our goal!*

I was performing at my peak. My toe-touch jump felt great.

My optional cheer wasn't an original, but one that I'd done a hundred times in Texas. As I finished I stood there with my hands on my hips, knowing I'd done my very best.

I hardly had time to climb back onto the bleachers before I heard Lauren's number called. I held my breath.

*Touchdown! Touchdown! That's our goal!*

The big gym echoed with the sound of her voice—low and loud and clear.

When Lauren finished, we all hugged and whispered congratulations to each other. I wasn't worried about the next part of tryouts—partner cheers. But what about the part after that? We hadn't talked about our group cheer at all this morning. But pretty soon, we were going to have to do it. And what were we going to do?

# CHAPTER
## 18

*H*ow could I have started too soon?" Tara wailed.

"Come on," said Lauren, grabbing Tara's arm and pulling her over toward the football field. It felt so good to be outside, away from the tension inside the gym!

"Listen, Tara," I said as we sat down on the bleachers, "the way you handled it was really super. The judges were impressed with your poise, I could tell."

"I agree," said Cassie. "Something like that can actually work to your advantage."

As we ate our lunch, we analyzed all the girls we thought had been really good. I knew four of the twelve we narrowed it down to: Kelsey McGee, Michelle Bostick, Emily Greer, and Darcy Lewis.

"Darcy *is* really good," said Lauren. "So's Emily."

"Yeah," agreed Tara. "They'll make the squad for sure." She shook her head. "That'll make me feel better if I don't."

After we ate, Lauren suggested walking around the track.

"Just to keep moving," she said.

"Go ahead," I told the others. "I want to sit here with old Brian Gilpin for a minute and think through the partner cheer."

As I watched them walk off toward the track, it hit me again how much I wanted us all to make the squad together. But after seeing the other girls this morning, I knew it would be hard. After all, there were only six places.

"How'd you do in there?" someone behind me said.

I turned and saw Drew Kelly standing by the bleachers.

"Okay so far," I told him.

"Um . . . you think," Drew said, "if it's not too much trouble or anything, that sometime I could see your dad's clippings?"

"Sure," I said. "My dad would love to show them to you."

"Your *dad?*" Drew's voice kind of cracked on the word. It sounded as if meeting Wild Bill in person might be too much!

"How'd you know we had a scrapbook, anyway?" I asked.

"Missy told me."

*"Missy?"* Now my voice cracked. "You know my sister?"

Drew nodded. "She always comes over to play with my dog."

"Your dog?" I said. "Your dog is . . . Spooky?"

"Right," said Drew, the boy next door. "Spooky."

Out of the corner of my eye I saw my friends standing on the track, staring over at us and whispering.

"I've got to go," I said. "Come over anytime."

"Thanks," said Drew. "See you."

I walked over to the track. Tara wouldn't believe that Drew lived right next door! I knew I'd have to put up with some teasing from her for talking to Drew. But I didn't care. At least it had taken my mind off cheerleading for a few minutes!

"When I call a number," Salleen said, "that girl should go to the center of the gym with her partner. If any stunts require additional spotters, please let us know. Okay, number one."

Darcy Lewis walked to the middle of the gym with Emily Greer. When Mrs. Holland gave the signal, they began:

*Excitement will be flowing!*
*A touchdown will occur!*

On the word *touchdown* Darcy lunged forward. Emily put her foot on Darcy's upper leg, and on the word *occur!* she kicked her other leg out to the side.

"Nice L-stand," whispered Lauren.

It wasn't as hard a stunt as a shoulder stand, but still, Emily was a flier. I thought they should have asked for a spotter just to be on the safe side.

Emily began her dismount on the words:

*There is no doubt!*

But as she came down, her foot twisted and she lost her balance. Everyone gasped as both girls toppled to the floor.

Steve Liu ran out to them.

"Lucky ducks," whispered Tara.

I could see both Darcy and Emily telling him that they were okay. He helped them up and they began walking off the floor. Emily was limping slightly. Darcy's face was red and angry. When they got to the side of the bleachers, Darcy must have thought that no one was paying attention to them anymore, because she turned to Emily and in a loud whisper said, "You total klutz! I can't believe you messed up that stunt!"

"That will be enough, number one," Salleen called over the loudspeaker.

With that Darcy made a sort of low growling noise and stomped out of the gym. Tryouts were over for her. Someone, I thought, should have given Emily some advice: *Keep practicing with Darcy and you won't stand a chance of making the squad.*

After that lots of girls asked for spotters—even when their cheers only had pony sits! When Cassie's number was called, she and I did our cheer the best we'd ever done it. Lauren and Tara were terrific too.

It was nearly three o'clock before group cheers started. Mrs. Holland handed out papers, all with the same cheer:

*Beware the Lions! You're up against the best!*
*Yes, we are the Lions! We'll put you to the test!*

132

"Whoever wrote this," Tara scoffed, "has no ear!"

"Never mind that," said Cassie, sounding slightly hysterical. "What moves are we going to put to it?"

We all pitched in with suggestions on how to show off our strengths. Only when we got to the last line did we hit a snag.

"We can't end it with a ripple," Cassie insisted. "You know what Mrs. Richardson said about our timing! And we haven't done a unison jump all week!"

"But we have to end it with *something* that shows we can work as a team!" said Lauren.

Cassie started sputtering ideas from her cheerleading books.

"Cassie," said Tara, looking her in the eye, "my jump in the individual cheer was the best I've ever done. I know we can do the flying split ripple. I won't let the team down."

As Mrs. Holland called that our ten minutes were up, Cassie barely whispered, "Let's go with the ripple, team."

Our group went seventh. As I stood there waiting, my heart was beating so hard underneath my yellow T-shirt that I thought maybe the judges could see it!

Cassie called loudly, "Ready, *and!*"

We went into action. Arms out in a T-motion, sharp and crisp. Back to half-T. Circle around. On the word *best!* Tara and I lunged forward, and Lauren jumped up on our thighs. After she hopped down, we moved quickly into formation for the ripple jump, the words of the cheer acting as our count. On the word *you* Tara jumped up, spread out her legs, and came so very close to touching her toes! Cassie went next, then me, and on *test!* Lauren finished up with a flying toe-touch jump that brought gasps even from the stone-faced judges. As we stood there with our arms up, catching our breath, we all smiled the kind of smiles that don't need any practice!

By five o'clock run-proof mascara was smudged on Tara's cheek and Cassie's frizzies had come back with a vengeance. Lauren's shorts had a tiny rip in the back and my T-shirt was wet under the arms. Our morning of beauty seemed far in the past.

None of the other girls sitting on the bleachers looked much better. Everyone was edgy. Out of the fifty-two girls who had come to tryouts, only six would go home completely happy. A seventh, the alternate, would go home semi-happy.

"Thank you all for trying out today," Mrs. Holland said over the loudspeaker. "Now, take your seats and the judges will announce the new seventh-grade cheerleaders. Please wait to come up to the judges' table until all the numbers have been called."

Cassie put out a hand and we all piled ours on top. Instead of popping them up, we held on to each other and hoped like crazy.

Mrs. Holland took a sheet of paper from Salleen. "The following will be the new Paxton Junior High cheerleaders: number seven."

A scream rang out in the gym. Kelsey McGee clapped both hands over her mouth and burst into tears. Much yelling followed.

"Please wait to applaud," said Mrs. Holland, "until I've called all six numbers." She looked at her list. "Number nineteen."

"That's Michelle," whispered Lauren.

Our hands pressed more tightly together.

"Number twenty-five," called Mrs. Holland.

Cassie!

"Number twenty-seven," called Mrs. Holland.

My heart flipped over. Twenty-seven! That was me! I'd made the squad. But number twenty-six hadn't. That was Tara.

Tara closed her eyes, and tears popped out at the corners. We squeezed our hands even tighter.

"Number twenty-eight," called Mrs. Holland.

Lauren!

None of us heard the last number. We just sat there, our eight hands in a pile, with tears running down our cheeks.

"Those are our cheerleaders," said Mrs. Holland. "Let's give them a big round of applause as they come up."

"Go on," said Tara. She tried to shake off our hands. "Go up there, before they change their minds."

Leaving Tara sitting by herself on the bleachers was about the hardest thing I'd ever had to do. I could tell Cassie and Lauren felt the same. Slowly we made our way to the floor and then walked over to the judges' table.

Salleen was grinning. "Congratulations, people!" she cried, and then took a closer look. "Why don't you look like girls who've just made cheerleader?"

"We're happy," Cassie said limply. "But sad for Tara."

Salleen sprang up suddenly and said something to Mrs. Holland. The cheerleading sponsor looked sort of flustered as she reached for her microphone. "A thousand apologies, girls," Mrs. Holland said. "I forgot to announce the alternate."

Instantly the room grew quiet.

"The cheerleading alternate is number twenty-six."

Tara! She'd made it after all. We all looked up into the bleachers and caught Tara's expression of disbelief.

Tara flew down from those bleachers then, and no one in the history of Paxton has ever heard such whooping and yelling and hollering as took place in the Paxton Junior High School gymnasium that afternoon. We'd all made it! Our whole team—together! We were Paxton cheerleaders!

# About the Author

KATY HALL grew up outside of St. Louis, Missouri, where she rooted for the Ladue High Rams. She has written four novels for middle grade readers and has collaborated with Lisa Eisenberg on more than twenty humor books for young readers, including *Batty Riddles* (Dial) and *The Family Survival Handbook* (Scholastic). Ms. Hall lives in New York City with her husband, daughter, and two cats, and enjoys attending plays and ballet performances.